Shadows on the Stage

A Performance of Prose and Poetry

Edited By Nadine Brito and Claire Wallace
Shadows on the Stage: A Performance of Prose & Poetry

Published June 2025

Poetry editing by Alice Eaves and Charlie Hilton
Typesetting by Salvör Sólnes
Typeset in Plantin MT Pro

ISBN: 978-1-907811-03-6

https://www.forestpublications.co.uk

Contents

An Intermission

Act IV

Act V

Curtain Call

Introduction

Life's but a walking shadow, a poor player,
That struts and frets his hour upon the stage,
And then is heard no more.

Macbeth V • 5

A Note from the Editors-in-Chief

There's nothing like the moment right before the beginning of a performance.

Whether you've gone to see any kind of show – a play, a film, a concert – there's always that moment of anticipation right before it starts. That moment when you take your seat, and sit back, your focus turning to the dark stage before you that will soon light up, transporting you to another world. In this moment you are excited for what's ahead, and you hear the intake of breath, feel the electric buzz in the air as you and your fellow audience wait. You are part of a community that shares the moment. As red curtains are pulled back, opening trailers start, or instruments begin to strum – the lights shift, and the darkness and shadows are transferred to the audience so they may see all that transpires on the stage.

Like the community we form as an audience, the performers on the stage share a community designed to make us feel, to empathise. The story the performers tell immerses us in their vision and imagination, sharing life from their own unique perspective. And the stage creates a liminal space in which to act it out upon. Similarly, the genres of horror, fantasy, and science fiction become a space where the realities, emotions, and psyche of humanity can be examined. In this way, genre is a performance unto itself.

Both of us have our roots in the film industry; Claire was raised in Los Angeles, a city that is entrenched in the culture of movies and television, and Nadine worked in the Canadian film industry in Toronto for a decade. Meeting in Edinburgh, rich in its own history of writing, performance and storytelling, was fortuitous. After many conversations and writing sessions over coffee, it was our friendship and shared history that inspired *Shadows on the Stage*, along with our mutual love and respect for stories in genre. We are excited to have found an international community of genre writers that have eagerly offered their own interpretation and perspective of performance.

Within this collection you will find short stories and poetry from a diverse array of writers coming from a variety of backgrounds. Not only do they write, but they are performers, musicians, dancers, visual artists, and more. Similarly, our team also reflects this range of creative expression. We are excited that we can present an anthology that represents the collaboration and community that performance and genre inspires.

We are pleased that you've decided to partake in this particular performance. Now please, sit back in your seat and enjoy the show.

Nadine Brito
& Claire Wallace

A Note from the Poetry Editors

Reading through the poetry submitted has been an honour, and a rewarding process as we see the myriad of ways in which our contributors have taken the prompt. Poetry is, by nature, an experimentation with the written word to push language, form, and ideas to their limits, discovering new modes by which they can be combined, torn apart, or reinvented. It is this defining attribute of poetry that gives it its performative nature.

When confronted with a poem, we are witnessing a performance. A performance of what? The poet? The speaker? Language itself? The form on the page? In truth, it can be all of these things, or none of them. What makes poetry a living and breathing thing is its ability to shift shapes and defy expectations – try to define poetry, and there will be something that works against that definition. Poetry is the thing in itself, in the same way, that a cube is the best definition of a cube. It is in this manner that the words of Isadora Duncan come to mind. When asked what a dance of hers meant, she responded: *if I could put it in words, why would I go to the effort of dancing it?* If we could tell you what a poem is, and what it means, then why would we go to the effort of writing poems and reading them?

All of the poets in this anthology demonstrate an innate understanding of this idea. Their work has taken our central concept, twisted and turned it in a way that can only be the workings of human creativity. In doing so, they demonstrate how poetry can be a glimpse into something more than the world we see before us. They are a reflection of what it means to be here, right now, as a human. They have brought the intangible into the material world. It is to this end that they operate as *Shadows on the Stage*.

Alice Eaves
& Charlie Hilton

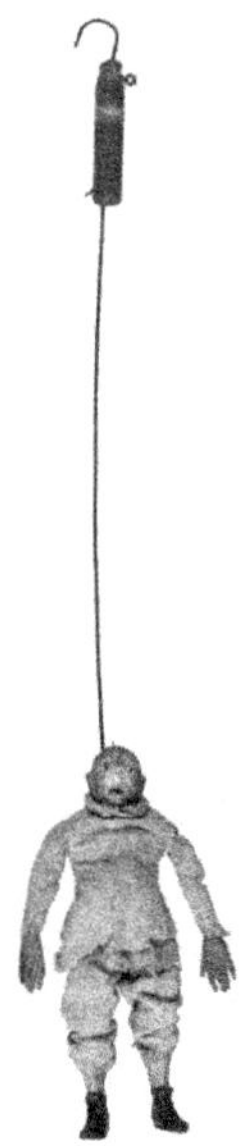

Act I

Finds tongues in trees, books in the running brooks,
Sermons in stones, and good in everything.

As You Like It II • 1

The Nuckelavee

Emry Beattie

Atop the shifting Shetland dunes
Amidst the scattered balding seagrass
I saw a portent of death and doom
Of horror not yet come to pass

This thing that I saw stood at the shore
Not daring to set foot on the land
With the sky and rain grim and dour;
On its back, what seemed a man

Or so I thought, in the dim light,
A lonely rider and his steed
But something there was not quite right
The way it stood amongst seaweed

I called out to this gloomy stranger
Picking my way down the scree
Not knowing the danger
For this creature was the Nuckelavee

A grim, fell omen the locals know
A demon from beneath the waves
Kept contained in summers glow
In winter's grasp it fills the graves

I could not know, I could not dream
The horror that now stood before me
When I first saw its face, I could not scream
This demon borne from the sea

It's fur, I thought, a dark red hue
Twisted muscle, fresh and bare
Its flesh a mass of writhing sinew
Glistened with salt in the cold sea air

The rider no man at all
But all one monstrous, twisted shape
A bloated head to reel and fall
Distended mouth to flap and gape

A horse's head, like no horse I've seen
A single eye of hate and bale
Mouth stretched wide with needle teeth
Its sickening grin like a whale's

From two foul mouths, miasma pours
A black, dense, acrid, choking smog
It's touch or smell all life abhors
Rots fields of grains to a bog

Disease decimates quaint island life
Young and healthy, sick and old
None go untouched from the monster's blight
And winter's chill cuts cold

I'm in bed now, to a life I cling
There's now none left to help me
Wishing I'd not seen that dreadful thing
That cursed fiend from the undersea

The horrid form of twisted life
The ghastly beast that all men flee
Omen of death, and bringer of strife
The monstrous and dreadful Nuckelavee

The Price

Jo Marjoribanks

The muffled sounds of the excited audience echoed through the wings of the theatre. They stretched all the way to the dressing room, itself a flurry of anxious activity. The contemporary dance troupe were preparing for their final performance. The previous four performances at Edinburgh's Festival Theatre had delighted and enraptured thousands, and they were eager to make this last one the most memorable.

Makeup brushes made pirouettes in multi-coloured palettes, sending clouds of fine powder billowing around cheeks that flushed with anticipation. The dancers who had finished their makeup stood away from the vanity mirrors, striking various poses around the room as they prepared their bodies for what lay ahead.

Only one person remained seated. Ostensibly calm and composed, Ava gently smoothed down a few errant strands of hair and slowly inserted another pin into her coiffure. Turning her head gingerly to the side, she evaluated her efforts with practiced poise. Ignoring the idle chatter of her fellow performers, she stifled a cough as a mist of hairspray drifted towards her through air that was already too thick and oppressive.

Only a few more minutes, Ava thought. As the principal dancer closing tonight's show, she would be afforded a brief period of solitude while the others performed the penultimate number.

Clenching her jaw, careful to avoid showing any sign of discomfort, she subtly shifted the position of her legs beneath the dressing table. Muscles that ought to have been supple and responsive fought against her brain's commands. Suppressing her frustration, she gripped the base of her seat for support and gently slid her right foot out from behind her left. A fusillade of tiny fireworks exploded along her nerves, showering her calves with painful sparks as her feet settled into their new position.

'Two minutes, folks!' Jeff rapped his knuckles against the door.

His exclamation caused a stir, and a flurry of fabric and palpable energy began making its way out the door. Skye paused as she passed by Ava's chair, her eyes alight with a mixture of excitement and nervousness. She smiled and rubbed Ava's shoulder encouragingly. 'Good luck out there. Not that you need it!'

Her well-meaning touch felt like sandpaper rubbed against sunburnt skin, and Ava fought to keep from flinching. She forced a breath through her nose as the grip on her seat tightened.

'Thanks, Skye,' she feigned a smile, 'break a leg.'

Skye chuckled, 'I thought we agreed that we abhorred clichés.'

'Fine,' Ava relented, 'how about "Dinnae fall on yer bahookie!"'

'Much better,' Skye grinned before gliding through the door in a whirl of glitter and exuberance.

The moment the door closed, Ava's mask fell away. A grimace marred her delicate features, and her fingers curled around the organza of her skirt, balling it tightly to expose the cobalt silk beneath. The shoulder where Skye's hand had been pulsed in an agonising rhythm, as if she had wished Ava good luck with a swift punch rather than a gentle touch. She reminded herself to breathe, but each inhalation seemed to awaken a sleeping serpent that wrapped itself around her ribs, squeezing harder until she felt she would pass out.

'You're on in five, Ava.' Jeff's voice sounded outside the door.

Through tightly drawn lips, she grunted a sound of acknowledgement and steadied one hand against the edge of the vanity.

The mirror jostled and for a moment she thought it would tip and shatter. But it remained in place, its polished surface offering her a glimpse of the real version of herself that she was so careful to keep hidden.

The next few minutes felt endless as Ava forced herself to move through the door and along the corridor towards the stage. Every step brought fresh waves of pain and unnerving sensations. A prickling heat in her right hand. A tingling cold along her spine. Black spots before her eyes. The thunderous applause sounded, signalling the end of the previous performance. She reached the edge of the stage just as the last of those dancers exited the opposite wing.

The applause began to trickle away as the audience waited in anticipation of her appearance. The stage was empty now, ready for her presence. The sight fortified her, subduing the serpent long enough to allow the flow of desperately needed oxygen into her lungs. Letting her eyes close, Ava's focus shifted beyond the physical.

In her mind, the stage was flooded with blue light. Swirling shades of sapphire and cerulean danced across its wooden surface and coalesced into a circle that encompassed the space, washing over the gilded cornices to give the appearance of sunset over a sparkling sea.

The theatre hummed with a primordial energy that made her heart beat faster as her feet propelled her forward. Just before she reached the boundary separating her from the expectant eyes of the audience, Ava whispered an ancient invocation. Her voice took on a reverent and lyrical quality as she called on the elements. Earth to ground her mind; fire to fuel her body; water to cleanse her pain; and air to carry it away.

Stepping onto the stage, it was as if the laws of gravity bent to her will. The struggle of her previous steps was replaced with a glorious feeling of weightlessness. She glided across her sacred space to take up a position at its centre. Raising her arms above her head, she smiled as her muscles yielded to her desire with no hint of agony or resistance. As the violinists drew their bows across their strings in the first flutters of musical movement, Ava inhaled a painless breath and began her dance.

Minutes drifted by in an ecstasy of movement and freedom. Only in this space could she be completely still, yet in motion at the same time. Only here could she find serenity, a sense of peace and liberation, where even her conscience was silenced.

In the darkness beyond the stage, in the centre stalls of the audience, a middle-aged man felt a sharp pain lance across his chest. Alarmed, he instinctively tried to raise his hand to clutch it, but found an unseen force preventing his movement.

In the front row of the dress circle, a young woman had a sudden, deep ache in her breast that seemed to throb in time with the whip of the dancer's fouettés.

In the upper circle, a teenage girl gasped as the sequined fabric of her dress scraped across her shoulder like a sharpened razor over delicate skin.

Panic and confusion rippled through the crowd. Though desperate to flee and escape this mysterious malady, their bodies were no longer theirs to command. Their unwilling eyes were pulled inexorably towards the stage where they fixated on the dancer lost in her euphoria.

The music built to a crescendo. Ava spun around in pirouette after pirouette, faster and faster, as if she could outrun the end of her performance and the inevitable return to reality. As the final notes from the grand piano sounded, her movements slowed, and she returned to the centre of the stage. She stood still for a moment, tears of joy and loss blurring her view of the rippling radiance of the circle that shielded her from pain.

Finally, she raised her right arm above her head, fingers outstretched, before sweeping it down gracefully to rest against her stomach. Dipping low into a bow, she felt a single teardrop slip down her cheek before striking the stage floor.

There was no sound of adulation from the audience, still held in place by the agony and fear they had been forced to carry. In the silence, her conscience began to stir. She couldn't linger any longer. Ashamed, she turned from the audience and walked slowly towards the boundary of her circle, pushing her guilt aside while she savoured the last moments of freedom. The delicate pass of her fingertips as they wiped away her tears did not burn her skin; the press of the soles of her feet against the wooden floor did not ache; the hitch of her breath as she fought back more tears did not fire daggers into her chest.

When she finally reached the circle's circumference, she allowed herself one final moment to enjoy every sensation. Forcing her eyes closed, she pulled in one last painless breath, and, with another whispered incantation, took back what she had willed away. This time, her voice was filled with regret and reluctance as she banished the elements one by one, and with them their temporarily granted protection.

The instant the last syllable left her lips, pain raced along every nerve in her body. It was so much worse than before, stealing her breath and blocking out all sight and sound, until she was only aware of the blood in her veins that felt as if it had turned to acid. Staggering forward, she grasped at the folds of the stage curtain to keep from falling. Knowing that she couldn't stay, Ava took a step, gasping at what felt like a knife thrusting into her chest, twisting in admonition for the violation of her audience. It was no less than she deserved.

Every night, Ava swore to the Goddess that this would be the last time. That she would never again force her pain on others for a few precious minutes of freedom. Yet every night she broke that promise, and as punishment her pain returned threefold the moment that she stepped off the stage.

Clutching the rich velvet of the curtain, she heard the carefree and rapturous laughter of her fellow dancers as they revelled in the joy of their art. And she knew, as surely as she knew that each step back to the dressing room would be torture, that she would keep paying this price. Her conscience would always succumb to her desire to dance without pain. Perhaps she could have resisted the temptation, were it not for the even stronger need she harboured.

The longing to be understood.

To have her suffering shared.

To not be alone in agony.

Was that so wrong?

On the Road

Bob Beagrie

Wretched, the hand curled up like a crumpled autumn leaf on the car's back seat, among backpacks and boxes of unsold CDs. The car is speeding along the A road, wind buffets the vehicle, rain spatters the window, and the wipers squeak squeak squeak like a snared rat. Each jolt brings a groan or a whimper from the fist's hidden palm. It is struggling to keep afloat in the ocean of red wine that sloshes beneath its skin. The skin that flushes like a cuttlefish in a heated debate about exactly how many bottles were drained last night after the gig. They ask the hand how it's feeling and chuckle, sharing recollections of its scandalous behaviour, oh and the things it said. *What, you don't remember?* they tease. The voices turn to other stories. The driver plans a pit stop for food and coffee. As the car pulls into a lakeside service station and they pile out onto puddled tarmac a blast of wind catches the hand as if it's an empty paper bag, sweeping it up, spiralling and tumbling across the choppy pewter waters toward whatever dwells in the vast forest.

Mina

Eleanor McMahon

Tasmin was muttering again, not that she knew it. It was usually a pointed tutting that alerted her that she was talking, once again, to herself, and that whichever Auntie had popped round to visit her Mum had noticed. It seemed all her Aunties were capable of doing was noticing things about her and tutting at them.

The nail biting, once it materialized, was quickly squashed; her Mum bought special nail polish that tasted like death and applied it liberally. Whenever Tasmin had the urge to gnaw at the tiny whites at the edge of her nails, she remembered the polish that was now a permanent resident in the bathroom cupboard.

The hair brushing had been a wearier battle. Tasmin was sure that when she was little no one had cared, sure that she remembered her Mum and Aunties smiling into their tea as she'd stormed in and out of the kitchen looking less and less like a girl and more like a thing that lives in a bush. It was unsettling then, when her appearance as she ran breathlessly back in from the garden stopped getting crinkled smiles, and instead got raised eyebrows, glances at her clothes, and straight lips.

One afternoon, in the autumn that she'd started big school, her Mum had sighed in a way Tasmin hadn't heard before, glanced at the Aunties and said, 'I just told you to give that hair a brush Tas.'

That's a lie, Tasmin had thought. *You're lying. You didn't just tell me. You haven't said that since this morning.* But she said nothing.

Then, not long after her eleventh birthday, as Tasmin bounced down the stairs, hair lovingly slept in, her Mum took one look at her and said 'If you don't want to brush it, fine. We'll just have to cut it all off. That'll stop the tangles. We'll go after school.'

And that was that. Hair cutting was non-negotiable. Tasmin was trying to grow it down to the floor. She skulked upstairs, brushed it, then stared at herself in the mirror. Her eyes felt hot. Tasmin lifted up her chin and puffed out her chest. She would face this injustice for now, but let it be clear, she was not happy about it.

But the muttering? The muttering persisted. She muttered at school, she muttered when she went to the little shop on her way home to buy sweets, she muttered as she ambled down the path that led to the woods on the outskirts of town.

What alerted her to her muttering this time, however, wasn't the teasing of the man in the shop who called her Tam-Tam (which she hated) and grinned at her (which she hated more), or her Mum's sighing, or her Aunties' tutting. What alerted her to the mumbled conversation she was having as she picked her way through the woods, sweets under her arm, was that something spoke back.

She stopped.

Glanced around. No one.

That's what she'd thought. No one comes down here. And it didn't sound like a person anyway, at least not a single voice. It was like a buzzing, but soft. She looked up at the powerlines that hung above the clearing in the trees. No, it wasn't them. Too far away.

'Hello?' She ventured, staring around at the trees, the moss, the grass.

Again, the sound, so quiet she wondered if it was just the noise of her brain working. But then she would have heard it before. It was coming from outside of her. Definitely.

'Who are you?' she tried, then frowned and corrected herself. 'What are you?'

The sound again, slightly stronger. Was it coming from beneath her? It sounded like it was. She looked down at her feet. Just ground. Tasmin carved a trench into the mud with her toe and kicked at a tuft of damp grass. Nothing happened.

She frowned again, sat down on an old tree stump and had a Haribo. She needed to think. As she chewed, a breeze shook the canopy of green above her, speckling her with the remains of the afternoon rain. She swallowed and cleared her throat.

'Are you the woods?' she asked, then jumped up. The buzzing had come from the rotting stump this time, so close she could almost make out words.

Tasmin winced. 'Sorry for sitting on you.'

The sound said something back. She assumed it said something like 'it's okay', but she didn't know for sure.

What was speaking to her? It was in the tree stump. And in the ground, lots of voices speaking as one… *Worms? They live in the ground. But they don't have mouths. Or do they? And do they live in trees?* Tasmin thought hard, trying to remember everything she had been taught at school about worms. It wasn't a lot. She didn't want to ask whatever it was if it was a worm, because if it wasn't a worm, it may be offended.

She'd make sure before she asked. That's what she'd do. Tasmin circled the stump, carefully inspecting it. There was a rotted, hollowed-out cavity near the ground on one side. She crouched down and squinted. The space inside was dark, except for the spongy white head of a mushroom peeking out. She paused. *A mushroom? They definitely don't have mouths.* Tasmin suddenly felt her shoes sliding on the damp ground. She reached out quickly to steady herself, grasping at the stump's wet black bark. It came away in her hand. She slipped backwards, landing on a patch of moss.

Tasmin scowled at the bark, then froze as it convulsed in her palm, fizzing into little pieces, turning into dark sandy powder and then tiny embers of light that sank into her skin.

'Oh,' she said, and the voices answered, and this time she heard them properly.

Tendrils of bright white light burst out from where she stood. They pulsed as they spoke to her. She watched as it webbed out, impossibly thin under her feet, into the stump, up and around some of the trees, and away from where she stood. The lights danced around her, and she stared until they had finished speaking, faded, and the woods grew dark again.

She brushed her hand on her top and decided it was time to head home.

'I'll see you tomorrow' she said. The voices answered, once again in a whisper.

When she got home, her Mum sighed and told her off for getting mud on her school shoes.

***

The next day she found her best friend Lucy in the playground and told her she had something very important to tell her and asked if they could speak alone.

'Of course, Mina,' Lucy said sincerely, and they went to a bench in the corner. Lucy called her Mina because Tasmin liked being called Mina. She liked it more than Tasmin, or Tas, and definitely more than Tam-Tam.

When her Mum had first heard the small blond-haired girl calling her daughter Mina, she had rolled her eyes. 'Your name is Tasmin, not Tasmina, that doesn't really work.'

'I think Tasmina is nicer than Tasmin,' Tasmin had argued.

'No, Tasmina sounds like Tasmanian Devil.' And her Mum went back to making dinner. Tasmin's fondness for the nickname grew.

Lucy blinked eagerly. 'Well?'

'I went to the woods after school yesterday, and I think something magic happened. I can show you if you come with me today?' Mina offered.

Lucy nodded. 'Okay. But I can't stay for long, I've got dancing at five.'

***

After school, the two girls raced to the woods, past the little shop, down the street, and under the pylons that cut across the woods like a scar.

Tasmin found the exact spot she had stood the previous day and put her bag down. 'This is where it happened.' The voices were there again, fizzing under her feet. 'Do you hear it?'

'No, hear what?' Lucy looked unconvinced.

'The voices.'

'I can't hear anything.'

'Wait.' Tasmin saw a small brown leaf on the ground and picked it up. It started eroding like before. 'Look, quick!'

Lucy peered at Tamsin's hand as the leaf disintegrated into particles of white light.

'It's me,' Tasmin told the voices, and the grass lit up underneath her. The voices asked who the other person was.

'My best friend, Lucy,' she replied. 'Don't be afraid.'

The voices chattered.

'What are you?' Tasmin asked, but the light faded, and the voices slipped away. She didn't catch the answer. She looked at Lucy, who was deep in thought.

'It was a web of light,' Lucy said eventually.

'Yeah.'

'I think it's mushrooms,' Lucy explained. 'I remember Mum watching this thing about how they're all linked with wires under the ground, all feeding on stuff, all connected.'

Tasmin hummed. Just as she'd thought. Really, she'd figured it out first, it was her who'd found the mushroom in the stump after all, but she decided not to say that because Lucy was being very kind and helpful, and she didn't want to seem ungrateful.

'Can I try?' Lucy asked.

'Sure.'

Lucy picked up another brown leaf and held it. Nothing happened. Lucy turned to her. 'It's just you. You must have a magic power that allows you to communicate with the mushrooms, and it's stronger when you feed on what they feed on. Maybe you're part mushroom.'

Tasmin nodded. That made sense. She took the leaf from Lucy, and it withered into nothing. The woods lit up.

'What is your name?' Tasmin asked.

The voices replied.

'What did they say?'

'I'm not sure if I can pronounce it.'

The two girls watched the lights flicker out. Lucy picked up her backpack. 'I've got to go. I've got dancing.'

'I'll walk back with you.'

'Okay.'

***

Lucy ran up to her the next day at school and shoved her phone in Tasmin's face. Tasmin wasn't allowed to take her phone to school, her Mum didn't trust her with it. Technically Lucy was supposed to keep it in her bag, but that had never stopped her.

'Look. I was right.'

Tasmin's eyes focused on the page. 'My-kel-aye-am.'

'Yeah. So like that's the body of the mushrooms, it's all underground and you don't see it. The actual mushroom bits are just like…like the fruit at the top.'

'What's that?' Tasmin and Lucy spun round. It was Becka, a stocky girl with glasses and mousy hair. Lucy and Tasmin looked at each other. She was a bit annoying but generally quite nice. And not very judgy. And last year she'd said she'd seen the ghost of her dead dog in her room. Tasmin smiled.

'Are you free after school?'

***

Becka stared at Tasmin's hand. 'So the magic comes from you absorbing plants?'

'Yeah. Think so.' Tasmin shrugged.

'Can you do anything else with it? Like if you had more?'

Tasmin hesitated, she hadn't thought of that. 'Maybe.'

As Lucy and Becka dumped fistfalls of dead leaves and moss at her feet, Tasmin stared at the stump. There was another mushroom peeking its head out from the crack near the bottom. *That wasn't there before, was it?*

'Try that,' Lucy stuttered, catching her breath, her cheeks tomato red.

Tasmin took some leaves and moss in her hand. The leaves burned away as before, but the moss remained. The voices clamoured all around her. Kicking off her shoes, Tamsin peeled off her socks, and let her bare feet rest on the ground. The voices were even clearer now. She smiled.

'Why just the leaves?' Becka asked.

The three girls thought in silence for a moment, watching the light dance around Tasmin's feet and shoot out in threads into the woods. After a while Becka sniffed and said, 'The leaves are dead. Maybe you're only absorbing dead things.'

Tasmin looked at the tree stump. *It was dead wasn't it? It was rotting. Does that mean it's* – Tasmin jumped as something thudded down in front of her. She stared at the large branch that lay at her feet.

'There was a fallen tree over there,' Lucy explained bluntly.

Tasmin nodded and gingerly touched it. The branch crumbled into ash, then dust, then finally light, brighter than any she'd been able to make before. The forest floor exploded with white filaments; the voices chimed crisp and clear. She breathed in and out, and the ground moved with her, flickering with her heartbeat, shuddering with every exhale. The voices made her smile. She giggled.

'What are they saying?' asked Becka. Lucy shushed her.

Tasmin looked over at a large rock to her left. She reached out her hand in its direction, and the tendrils under the ground shot towards it. Slowly the rock began to glow too.

***

'Will I need to tell Mr Hughes to stop selling you sweets before dinner?'

Tasmin glanced up from the cobweb looking thing she'd been doodling along the edge of her maths jotter. Her Mum was brandishing an empty Haribo packet at her. Her Aunties tutted. Tasmin shrugged and went back to her drawing. Her Mum stood up from the washing basket.

'Tasmin, I'm talking to you. Shall I see what he thinks?'

Tasmin muttered and connected two dots with a razor-sharp line of pencil.

'What was that?'

Tasmin huffed and repeated herself, louder this time. 'I said, I don't care what he thinks. He's weird.'

Tasmin's Mum glanced over at the Aunties. The women looked at each other. Tasmin looked between them. What had she done now? Eventually her Mum turned to her, went to say something, but she didn't. Instead, Tasmin watched as her Mum walked over to the bin, threw the empty packet away and went back to the laundry. Her Mum was gnawing at the skin on her lip. Tasmin scrunched up her face, and decided next time to just stay quiet.

***

A group of girls approached her and Lucy the next day at lunch, Becka trailing after them.

The tallest, Samira, cleared her throat. 'Can you show us?'

Tasmin looked up from her cheese sandwich. 'Show you what?'

'The magic. Becka said that—'

Lucy threw a scornful look at Becka.

'—I'm sorry!' Becka fumbled. 'I just thought…it was amazing…I had to say.'

'It's okay,' Tasmin said. She couldn't blame her. It was.

'Will you show us?' Samira asked again.

'Just you three?'

'Well,' Samira looked at the other two girls, 'I think the other girls in class were wanting to see too…'

'All the girls in class?' Lucy sniffed. She frowned and looked at Tasmin.

Tasmin shrugged. 'Sure. I think they should see it. The whole class.'

'Even the boys?' Lucy wrinkled her nose.

The six of them pulled faces.

'No. They would just ruin it,' Tasmin said, and the other five nodded. They would.

***

Tasmin's Mum sighed as another plaited grass bracelet fell from her daughter's school jacket. Tasmin quickly picked it up and shoved it back into her pocket. Her Mum raised an eyebrow.

'It was a gift.'

'And that's very lovely, but maybe you should keep all these… gifts somewhere else?'

That was going to be difficult. Her school bag was stuffed with trinkets, woven bracelets, drawings, twigs, rocks scratched with other rocks to make pictures, and so on. Gifts from the other girls. Talismans. Tasmin appreciated them greatly. The stump had become a shrine of sorts, and Lucy organised it all with military precision, vetting every gift. People brought offerings for the ritual too, and again, Lucy was in charge of figuring out if it was something that Tasmin could consume.

They'd tried a lot of things by now. It was Sarah who had realised it was similar to compost. and had then brought a whole tupperware container of onion skins. Tia had brought fallen apples from outside her Gran's house. Some girls took it upon themselves to keep the area tidy, brushing away debris from the stump and moving rocks. Others created a special drink by collecting rainwater in bottles and adding flower petals, which they all drank while watching the lights.

***

Whoever brought the dead mouse never owned up to it.

Tasmin was taking her hair out of its plait and skipping to the clearing when Lucy ran towards her.

'Mina, don't be upset. I don't know who brought it.'

'Brought what?' Tasmin asked as she neared the group. The girls stood in a circle around the stump. They parted to let her through, a few shifting uncomfortably. Tasmin approached the shrine. The top of the wood now bursted with little white mushrooms. Framed by this bulbous ring was a small furry brown body, its tail tucked underneath.

'It's so gross. You don't have to. It's horrible!' Lucy insisted.

Tasmin looked at the little creature. It was so still. The group watched her.

'You don't have to. Honestly,' Lucy insisted again, her eyes fixed on the mouse.

'It's okay.' Tasmin walked up to her place, and kicked off her shoes and socks. Lucy exhaled and smiled encouragingly, then gestured to the other girls. On her cue they all eagerly sat in a circle around the stump and waited. Tasmin sat down and stared for a moment at the little fuzzy body. Then she took a breath, and placed her right hand on its soft fur. Her eyes closed.

She saw the endless darkness of the earth. And then the light; hundreds upon thousands of threads thin as spider silk, a bolt of lightning forking out into the black, a nerve electrified in pain, stretching far, far away, further than she could have ever imagined. Reaching out, chattering, breathing, beating, blistering white hot, and beautiful, so, so beautiful. She felt herself reach out towards an unlit area, and the lights snaked their way over, filling it with a sparkling cobweb. As it filled, her senses sharpened ever more, as if she'd dived into a cold pool.

It was a map, a glowing living map, and she thanked the voices, and they thanked her back and told her they'd waited so long to show someone.

When she opened her eyes, the first thing she noticed was that someone had sliced the sky into diamond-shaped pieces.

She blinked. She was lying on her back, staring upwards at the pylon wires that cut across the grey-white sky. Her back was all wet. The girls hoisted her up. Lucy handed her the special water and told her how the whole ground had lit up. Samira said that even they had felt the buzzing. Becka told her how they heard the voices chattering through Tasmin's own mouth. Maria swore she saw her hair floating as if charged with static. Nell said she'd drooled. Lucy elbowed her. Tasmin didn't mind. Nell often said things that weren't very kind to get attention (her parents were getting divorced).

Tamsin looked over at where she had directed the lights. A tree stood there. She saw nothing now, but she knew in a few days she'd see tell-tale white dots on its surface, just as they'd appeared on the rock before. The rock had cracked. In a few weeks, it would erode completely and become soil. She could turn anything to soil.

If she wanted to.

She could light up the world.

***

Mr Hughes grinned as he saw her approach.

Little Tasmin Nandi, she hasn't come in a while. The bell jingled, and he leaned over the counter in anticipation. He'd wait until she came up with her Haribos, then he'd say, 'Anything else Tam-Tam?' or, 'That's a tenner please Tam-Tam.' She hated that one. Or maybe—

'How much?'

Mr Hughes grinned and looked up. His smile dropped. The girl's hair snaked around her shoulders, dark coils that shifted as if moving by themselves.

Had she gotten taller? He thought. *She seemed taller.* And her eyes. Something was wrong with her eyes. He knew what her eyes were meant to look like. Big, dark, just like her mother's. He liked her eyes . But now, they were paler, grey – no, not grey, white. He checked himself. *They must have always been grey. That's it. And the light must be—*

'How much?' She stared at him.

He looked away. 'One pound please.'

She placed the coin on the counter and left. Mr Hughes watched her stroll away. *Next time her mother comes in, I'll have a word*, he decided. Something wasn't right. He looked round the empty shop, shivered and decided to close early.

It was a Friday, after all. And he didn't want to be caught out if the power went again. The months of blackouts had made him anxious. It was getting darker earlier now, and you couldn't risk having the shop open in the dark with no power. 'Yes, better safe than sorry,' he mumbled to himself, and went to close the shutters.

***

The congregation beamed at her as she entered the clearing.

'Greetings Mina.'

'Greetings friends.' Mr Hughes had irritated her, but it was a Friday, and her congregation deserved a treat. She handed the sweets to Lucy. 'For after.' They had work to do first. Lucy nodded.

'Of course, thank you Mina. We found these.' Lucy nodded to the two small birds that sat on the shrine.

'Lovely. Thank you, Lucy.' Two birds would be plenty. Part of her had hoped for another rabbit, but it was only a matter of time. She had all the time in the world.

Mina gazed at the girls, barefoot, hair loose, adorned with twigs, flowers, and moss. The voices purred in her ear. She smiled and kicked off her shoes.

'I know,' she said. 'We do.'

The Fairies of the Forest

Megan Nicholls

The first thing we knew was darkness. Our supple limbs stretched out, reaching for each other, reaching for connection, and slithering through soil we threaded together. We held each other through the long night and drank life from the ground as we grew. We were content swaddled in the earth until the tapping began.

It was quiet at first, the *tip-tap* of rain drop footsteps, a light splattering of groups gathering, until it became a pattering, a rhythmic rattling. There was something about the drumbeat that drew us from our soft cocoon. So, we grew taller and taller, and our threads grew thicker until the tips of our heads pushed through the sky of our ever-shadowed world.

We lived before in a tactile world; we had never seen the green cushions of moss or the tinctured gold of sunlight on the forest floor. The threads of us below the soil clutched each other as we peered at our new home.

'They've awoken,' a tinkling voice said. The creature that stood before us sparkled and shone like nothing we could have fathomed in our world beneath the dirt. They glimmered above us, adorned with petals, leaves, and crystalline wings.

'I am Buttercup Fairy and we are the fairies of this forest,' said the creature dressed in the petals of the most colourful flowers in the glade. She stood before us with pointed toes, leaning down until her body almost folded in half to become level with the bobbles that bloomed at the ends of our limbs. 'We have given you life through our dance. Your little hat-like heads shall get bigger and your stems longer: one day you shall be much taller than us, as we too are only little. We shall call you mushrooms, and we shall be friends for ever and ever!'

We loved the fairies from the moment they twirled us into being and watched their ethereal beauty as we grew larger. We encircled their revelling and joined their song.

'My, my, how you've grown,' Sir Beetle said to us, as he clattered along in his iridescent armour. 'Very admirable work Buttercup Fairy, I must say!'

Buttercup Fairy sat upon his broad, opalescent back and smiled serenely. 'Yes, they're coming along very beautifully!'

We preened at her words, for we were then the same height as her.

We grew through rains, through sun, and through wind; we grew as we swallowed nutrients from the earth and absorbed the magic of the fairies' dance and song. We sent joy to each other, crackling through our fibres and fizzling up our fleshy limbs and our widening heads.

Buttercup Fairy came over to us one morning, grinning from ear to ear.

'You're growing so well that the King and Queen will honour you with a dance!' She beamed, the petals of her dress flowing about her.

We were overjoyed as the nighttime approached; the fairies sang flowers into bloom and illuminated our glade with fireflies. By the time King Frog and Queen Toad arrived, our circle of moss was ablaze with life.

'How marvellous!' Queen Toad exclaimed as she made her way around our circular walls, holding the plumes of her ballgown with her webbed hands. 'You have all grown so tall, you're nearly as large as our castle on the pond!'

In truth, we towered above all our local creatures, so much so that we nearly reached the height of the squirrel that sometimes lurked beyond the boundaries of our bodies.

'Indeed,' said King Frog, 'they will make perfect dwellings for your community, Buttercup Fairy.'

Buttercup Fairy looked delighted and so were we. We watched as the fairies fed their amphibian guests an unforgettable feast. They groaned and swooned with delight as they ate and ate and cried, 'Oh my! You grow the most delicious delicacies, Fairies of the Forest!'

We felt the pleasure we knew the fairies must feel at the compliment. They were such attentive hosts, and despite the utensils laid out for them, never even ate a morsel themselves!

Later that night King Frog bowed before the Queen, his little gold crown sturdily stuck to his head, and took her hand. They waltzed until morning, round and round the glade, and with them we swayed until we dropped drowsily to sleep.

The next morning, as the mist cleared from the forest floor, the aftermath of the feast laid before us. We had not seen as the fairies, with their tummies rumbling, tucked their napkins into the necks of their dresses and took up their teensy knives and forks. We did not feel as they pricked our surfaces with their forks, mouths drooling, and sawed back and forth with their knives, carving out mouthfuls of our flesh. We did not see the little serrated edges of their teeth or the points they had filed them into. They ate even more voraciously than the King and Queen had!

Overnight, our bodies had hollowed. Had been gnawed away to form windows and doors, and within, tables, chairs, warm fireplaces and beds, in which a fairy dwelled.

'Oh, it's been so long since we had a home!' The fairies cheered from their toasty beds rubbing their bulging little stomachs with their perfectly manicured hands. 'We love you for all you've done for us, dear mushrooms.'

We tried to reach out, stretch our threads to one another, but we could no longer feel under the ground, could no longer feel each other.

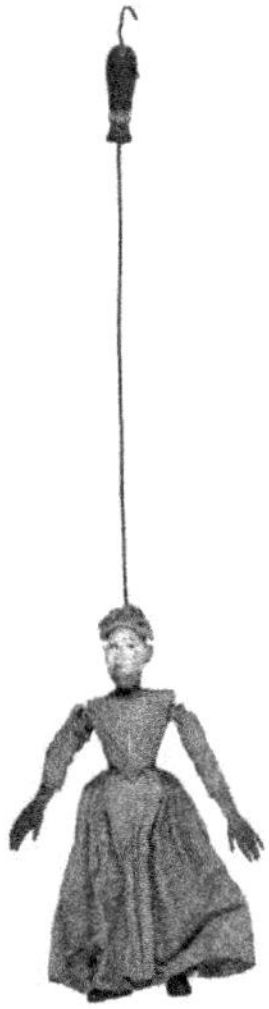

Act II

This above all: to thine own self be true.

Hamlet I • 3

An Amputation

Lily M. Frenette

Groggy, I wake.

The anesthesia has worn off too soon. The doctors' white coats float above me. They are oblivious to my searching eyes. I try to speak, to warn them, but my mouth remains still. My head is strapped tight to the table, and it is too numb to shake.

My eyes dart to all corners. The operating table is sunken down, and seats rise about me in circles. The doctors pause at different moments of the surgery, giving speeches to my spectators. There's polite applause.

My arm tickles. I hear the creaking of metal and glance in my periphery. A saw pulls back and forth across the tree trunk that is my arm. My shoulder leads to a strong oak. It has been strapped down perpendicularly to me. My stomach heaves at their distance.

The saw stutters in its rhythm. The toll of pushing it through my arm overwhelms the doctor. Sweat pools on his brow, dripping down onto my bark, flowing along the rivers of my skin. The doctor continues dragging the flimsy saw through my insides. I wish I could feel the pain, but the anesthesia seems to have worked in this one aspect. The sawdust piles onto the floor.

He calls for another doctor to relieve him. The new man appears, strong in his movements, pushing and pulling fluidly. He uses the full length of the saw. I watch him work for an hour until he too begins to tire. The saw is only halfway through.

It takes another two doctors to reach the bottom of my arm. Only a sliver of wood remains connected. After a quick consultation, they set aside the saw and instead, push the trunk down forcefully, snapping it off my shoulder. They hold it up like a trophy. The spectators applaud raucously.

They bring my trunk to an old man with a long grey beard. There are thousands of wrinkles on his face and arms. Grabbing his axe, he cleaves off my bark in long strips. He sits on a bucket, trapping my tree between his legs and whittles. His knife is curved, and it knocks tiny petals of wood to the floor. He sings as he works, folk tunes falling from his lips.

The upper arm is shaped first. It is given the slight swell of a bicep, but nothing significant. He labors over the elbow for ages, marking each crinkle and fold of skin. The forearm he pulls out in smooth strokes, and my wood curls like ribbons.

The hand takes his full concentration. He switches from singing to a soft hum. Starting with the pinky, he details the knuckles and nails. Ring, middle, pointer. Each is crafted with precision. For the thumb he uses a special tool. It must have a movement that the others do not. He taps it against each digit. When he gets to the palm of the hand, he holds it to his ear and listens. The room is silent as they wait. Then he nods and, with a pocket knife, cuts ley lines onto the palm.

He finishes and smoothes his hands over his work. The doctors rush over and snatch the arm away. To the excited audience, they demonstrate how it bends. A young man emerges with a bucket of paint. He watches as they hang the arm up, and cracks open the lid, dipping his brush into the varnish. The lacquer is applied in smooth strokes. Bowing, the young man leaves. I watch as the varnish drips down the arm's fingers.

A child enters with a broom, sweeping my pieces together into the fireplace. He lights the wood, and a warm smoke fills the air. It reminds me of home and darkness. My eyelids are heavy as a mountain of snowfall. They fall shut and I see the forest, smell the scent of oak fresh in my nose. Tears dribble down my face. My mouth finally breaks free of the anesthesia, and I gasp for air.

When the stain on the arm dries, a nurse begins to stitch it to my shoulder. She whispers platitudes in my ear as the heavy black thread goes in and out. Water drips onto my collarbone. I open my eyes and find her crying as well.

She ties the last stitch off with a square knot, then helps lift me off the table. The doctors crowd around, moving the arm this way and that. They murmur and nod to each other before spreading out so I'm visible to the audience. The head doctor steps forward and asks what I think. I lift up the wooden arm, comparing it to my arm of flesh and bone.

'It's perfect,' I cry. 'Exactly as it should be.' The audience cries with me through thunderous applause.

Splinters

Marco Etheridge

The venue is a vaulted basement, more subterranean burrow than theatre, where unlucky patrons purchase shelter from the pelting rain and scant hope of entertainment in equal measure. The stage is empty except for a single microphone stand, a tall wooden stool, and a pedestal table. Behind the stage hangs a threadbare curtain that might once have been a shade of burgundy, now mottled to various hues of brown.

Rows of tattered seats confront the stage. Not a full house. Many seats remain empty. The audience shifts and settles. Wet overcoats steam. Someone coughs into a muffling hand. A tearing sound as a well-worn sole pulls free from a sticky puddle.

The house lights flicker and die. A shaky spotlight illuminates the empty stage. A disembodied voice crackles from the darkness.

'Good evening, ladies and gentlemen. Welcome to the Grand Illusion. And now, please give a warm welcome to our star, Paolo Pinewood.'

A rail-thin man enters from stage right to a smattering of applause. Paolo Pinewood, a scarecrow in a black suit. He is clean-shaven, a man in his mid-thirties, perhaps, yet his face is smooth as a boy's.

His most notable feature is his nose. The startling proboscis is a beak-like appendage more suited to a wading bird than a human being. The man stalks across the stage, his nose leading the way, the sleeves and pant legs of his suit flapping over stick-thin limbs. He perches himself atop the stool, places a glass of water on the pedestal table, then raises his face to the audience.

'Buonasera, good evening, welcome. Before we begin, I must offer a warning. Anyone expecting technicolour cuteness, crickets, songs about wishes and stars, or a moral, will be gravely disappointed. I would ask you to leave the theatre. Now. Immediately. Your money will be grudgingly refunded by the troll masquerading as a human, who lurks in the ticket booth. No? No one? Very well, but please remember I warned you.'

A dramatic pause, a sip of water. And then...

'My name is Paolo Pinewood. Yes, the same as the famous movie studio. No reference to trees, I beg you, nor to wood. I came to life in this world in the year eighteen eighty-three.'

Murmurs from the audience, indignant rustling, a shifting of feet. The man on stage raises a bony hand.

'Please. I know many find this difficult to believe, but I assure you every word I speak is true. I am quite incapable of telling an undetected lie. This nose you see upon my face is, to speak kindly, prominent. Should I utter an untruth, my nose will grow most noticeably. Allow me to demonstrate.'

Paolo Pinewood turns his profile to his audience. He projects his firm voice to the back row of the theatre.

'There is no injustice in this beautiful world of ours.'

In an instant, the already protruding nose sprouts four additional inches of fleshy beak. The audience gasps. Paolo gives the crowd a sidelong smirk, then turns his eyes forward.

'Gravity binds us to this sad earth.'

The nose retreats to its former dimensions. Paolo turns to face the darkened seats.

'You see? If I tell the simplest lie, you will know it in an instant. Now, to continue, I came to life one hundred and forty years ago. I was not born. Rather, I was animated. I had no dear mother, only an aging father, a humble and lonely carpenter. Perhaps you have heard his name. He was called Geppetto.'

Paolo knows his audience. He is a veteran performer, after all. He pauses to let this new fact sink into their thick heads. A moment more, a sip of water, and he is ready.

'Yes, good, kindly Geppetto. For is that not how he is remembered? Whereas I, who once answered to a different name, am remembered as a rascal, even a rogue. Why, Geppetto himself called me a wretched boy. But let me caution you, my good friends. Events viewed through the blurred lens of history may not have occurred exactly as recalled.'

Paolo rises from his perch and steps to the edge of the stage. He spreads wide his thin arms, beseeching his audience.

'The real story, the true story, is this. Geppetto was a failure, a poor man alone and old. He had no wife, no children.

'To ease his loneliness, Geppetto carved scraps of wood into limbs, feet, hands, a head, a face with a grotesque nose. He joined those pieces together to form a life-sized puppet, then attached strings to this pitiful creation. By manipulating the strings, the old wretch forced the poor, lifeless puppet to caper around for his amusement.

'Harmless enough, you say. A decrepit codger and his new playmate. Perhaps, had he stopped there. But Geppetto wanted more. Desire and loneliness are powerful forces when joined.

'Geppetto wished for a living son. Wishes repeated often enough, and with sufficient fervour of belief, may take on a magic of their own. And so it came to pass that a lifeless marionette became something marvellous, a puppet who walked and talked and danced without the need of strings or a puppeteer. Yes, truly marvellous, but not human. A puppet still – made of wood – not a real boy of flesh and blood.'

The thin man drops his arms to his side, executes two stork-like strides backward, and perches once more on his stool. He lowers his head as if contemplating past sadness, but when he raises his mournful face to the audience, his eyes spark with anger.

'I am remembered as a rapscallion, a bumbler, and a boy prone to telling lies. But think! I was brought into this sad world as a child of nine but with no prior experience of the world. I was not raised in slow steady stages, nor taught how a hot stove burns the unwitting hand. Of course, I misbehaved. Is it any wonder? I possessed no more experience than a newborn babe, yet I was damned for mistakes that any baby would make.

'I was a naïf, thrown into the hard arena of life without knowledge or skills. Show me a naive innocent, gentlemen and ladies, and I will show you a pitiful creature that causes the villains of this world to lick their chops in anticipation. Indeed, I had my faults, but I also had my tormentors. Fox and Cat were my enemies. They dogged my steps, tricked me, humiliated me, and led me astray.'

Paolo Pinewood sags on his stool, casting forth a cloud of practiced despair to hover over the audience.

'Geppetto was not the only slave to wishes made upon stars. I myself came under the spell. Not content with my state, I wanted more. One wish, uttered again and again. A real boy, a boy of flesh and blood, let me become a real boy. How little I understood. That fervent wish would become my destiny and my doom.

'You no doubt know what happened next. I promised the Fairy with Turquoise Hair that I would do everything in my power to transform myself. I ran away from my home, from Geppetto, my father in name. My long journey led me to the Land of Toys. Instead of becoming a human boy, I was changed into a donkey, a lowly beast of burden. In despair, I joined a circus. As if these were not curses enough, I escaped the body of an ass only to be once again a wooden puppet.'

Paolo lets loose a long sigh and raises his hands to the darkened theatre.

'I'm afraid the final act of my little tale is the most contrived ending imaginable. My rescuer appears in the form of Geppetto, who somehow searched the world and found me. Then, in the nick of time, we were all swallowed by a gigantic fish, a flagrant use of deus ex machina stolen directly from the bible.

'Home at last and safe once more, the Fairy with Turquoise Hair came to me in a dream. Yes, friends, the dreaded dream sequence, that hackneyed tool of Hollywood scripts. What apology can I offer? I was merely a character, not the author, a wooden chip floating on the current of this wretched tale.

'But now to our happily ever after. I was changed, once and for all, into a flesh-and-blood boy. Cue the happy melody and the cheerful twittering of birds. Except this is not the end of my story, for magic is a fickle mistress. We have reached the end of the tale as you know it, an old familiar chestnut. But allow me to tell you more. Let us enter the later chapters of my life, which you've paid good money to hear.'

The stage fades to a dull glow. A thin figure in shadow, Paolo rises from his stool, slips the suit jacket from his narrow shoulders, and drapes it over the empty stool. He steps to the edge of the stage, unbuttons the cuffs of his shirt, and folds the sleeves back over broomstick wrists.

The spotlight grows brighter in a series of sudden pulses. The pool of light jerks to the left, swerves past its target, then veers back, finally pinning the actor where he stands. Paolo offers a mocking half-bow, then cups his hands to his mouth.

'Well done, Guido!'

Throws an aside to the audience.

'You must excuse Guido. He does his best with the one arm.'

A half-hearted chuckle from the crowd. Another tough room. They all are, these dingy, third-rate theatres. Most certainly not the Strand, but these rubes paid their dime. Paolo rubs his hands together with a flourish. Time to deliver the goods, such as they are. Time, yes, the very word.

'Magic, ladies and gentlemen, is a powerful force. You need look no further than my beak of a nose as an example. Yet magic is not the only power in this beautiful, sad world. Time waits for no puppet, no old man, and no magic.

'And so, we take up our tale at the supposed happy ending. The Fairy with Turquoise Hair, her duty done, moved on to other projects. I do not blame her. She had other mortal lives to attend to.

'Time marches on, but not in the same way for all things. A

tree ages over a century, but a human grows old in mere decades. Geppetto's flesh and blood were not crafted of magic. Nor were Cat and Fox. Time gnawed at them, and they died, one by one.

'I was left alone, without father, friend, or enemy. Yet lest any call me bitter, know that I hold no grudge against Geppetto. He did his best. His loneliness brought me forth. And who among us is not lonely in the long black night?

'Two decades passed, yet I aged no more than a handful of years. To human eyes, I seemed a teenage orphan. No matter my appearance, I was alone and hungry. To earn my daily bread, I joined a traveling minstrel show. I learned the craft of slapstick, pantomime, juggling, all the usual farcical fare.

'Sleight of hand became my stock and trade. I juggled seven balls at one time while bouncing an eighth on my nose. No small feat, I assure you. And after the show, my quick hands might lift a purse or two. I am not proud of this, but itinerant jugglers earned only a pittance.

'Thus, I wandered with the wagons, but I could not stay ahead of time or magic. I am forever cursed by both. Other players aged naturally, but not I. The denizens of stage and circus are a superstitious lot. Suspicions led to mutterings and mutterings to threats. They called me unnatural, a changeling, the son of witchcraft.

'And so, I took my leave one night, a sack of purloined goods slung over my shoulder. Just enough to sustain me upon my dark road, I assure you. I travelled far, found another minstrel show, and was hired on the spot.

'This pattern continued for many years; one show replaced by another. I existed in a circle of merry players, yet always alone, without friends or love. For there are other things, darker things, which magic cannot alter. And now the time has come to tell you of these.

'When old Geppetto carved my body from scraps of wood those many years ago, he fashioned a puppet. There was no thought in his grey head that I might one day spring to life. Hence, he neglected certain anatomical details. Yes, I have hands, feet, limbs, a head, eyes that see, ears that hear, and a truly magnificent nose. At first glance, one might consider me normal. But a crucial item is missing. What I lack is genitalia.'

A rustle washes through the darkened crowd. Paolo knows his audience from long experience. It is time to set the hook and reel them in. He waits, one heartbeat, two. An indignant voice shouts from the back rows.

'Prove it then!'

Tonight's shill is good, his timing perfect. Paolo smiles to himself. A few coins slipped into a greedy hand, a small price to move the show along.

Paolo shouts down his paid heckler.

'You doubt me?'

More cries from the audience now, the others joining in as they always do, night after night. Paolo drops his head as if in shame. He waits until the audience falls silent. Then he raises his eyes and glares.

'Very well. But remember, it was you who forced my hand.'

The denouement is swift and sure, a feat performed a hundred times and more. One hand to the waistband of his trousers, a pinch and a zip. The right hand pulls the loosened trousers down while the left sweeps the white shirttail aside. The spotlight gleams over the star's naked crotch, nether regions as unadorned as a girl's doll.

A gasp whistles from the crowd. Those patrons in the front rows push themselves back in their seats, turn their heads, but cannot avert their eyes.

There is no escape. Paolo Pinewood swings his barren groin a quarter turn stage-left, then a quarter stage-right, and once more to centre. The landscape between his belly and the top of his thighs is empty. There is no hair, no shaft, no scrotum, nothing but pale skin as smooth as polished wood.

Paolo hides his naked secret with practiced sureness. Before the crowd can regain their lost composure, he has lifted, zipped, and tucked himself back into a state of proper dress. His lips curl in a lurid smirk. He holds this audience in the palm of his hand, and he knows it.

'Now that we have removed all doubt, a small feat of magic. I will conjure answers to the questions you dare not ask. I told you I existed without friends or love. But I did not say I was devoid of sexual desire. All humans and most creatures on earth are driven by the powerful stimulus of lust. Some call it the urge to procreate. In that regard, I am no different than you, my friends. I lust for the pleasures of the flesh. Oh, how I lust.

'While it is true that I cannot receive sexual pleasure in the traditional fashion, I am not without means to provide the same. Oh, now I see your puzzled looks. You're asking yourselves how is this possible? The poor wretch lacks the essential gear. The answer to your confusion is that I compensate. It is my nose, you see, which comes to my rescue.'

Paolo Pinewood turns in profile, leers out of the corner of his eye, and gives his audience an exaggerated wink.

'Recall my earlier demonstration if you will. I lie, my nose grows. I tell the truth, my nose shrinks. I love you, I hate you. I hate you, I love you. The order of the words does not matter. The result is the same, only the rhythm changes. In and out; out and in. Think of that, then, as my substitute for the normal way of performing the act.

'But normal is such a false word, is it not? What I mean to say is, who amongst us is truly normal? Look to your left, to your right. Do you truly believe that not one of your fellow patrons is above a small deviance, a wobble away from the straight and narrow? And what of ourselves? Are not each of us capable of something more, or far less, than the accepted norm?'

He pauses at the edge of the stage, lets his words fan the unease of the audience. He senses the fear of disclosure oozing up and down the rows like a spilled soft drink. So many skeletons out there beyond the spotlight, an entire graveyard of sordid bones hidden in many closets.

'Fear not, folks. We are all consenting adults of a certain age. There is no need to be embarrassed. Your secrets are safe with me. That was our arrangement, was it not? Our little contract. You paid your entrance fee in the coin of the realm. That same payment obliges me to spill my guts onto this humble stage, while your dark secrets remain safely locked away. And so it shall be, gentlefolk. A fair contract, spit in the hand and shake on it.

'Done is done, but before I bid you adieu, I must confess to one small lie, an untruth so subtle as to remain undetected even by my over-sensitive hooter. At the beginning of tonight's entertainment, I warned you not to expect cuteness, silly songs about stars, or a clear moral.

'In this last item, I fear I misled you. There is a bit of a moral to my sordid tale, and it is this. When you wish upon a star, ladies and gentlemen, make certain you truly, deeply desire that for which you wish. And if you dare to wish, be clear, be exact, and don't blame me if things turn out for the worse.'

Without another word, Paolo Pinewood bends himself in the middle, bows almost to the boards, and backs across the stage. As he disappears behind the curtain, the end of his nose is the last thing the audience sees.

Sonata Form

Olivia Thomakos

Alone, you question the sanctum
that is your body, but without their lyrics you
are still symphonies. Your bass drum heart,
your eyelash cymbals, ebony keys
freckle your ivory keyboard.

They will practice and practice and practice
but you are Carnegie Hall,
and without them you will house performances.
Your hair sings the strings of violins, nose brass section
calling forward passersby.
You are music

and you were before they were listening.
They did not speak your song into being – your breath
always on key. Mouth made of flutes,
of piccolos, clarinets: soft and sweet
sinking others

into silence. Your body has been criticised,
blasphemed, veil torn in two,
but do not forget your troves of embroidered
tapestries and gold cups. You are made
of mosaics –

invite whom you like to this sanctuary
to praise the joyous noise that you are,
have always been. We do not
pray to make God exist.

Prima Donna

Claire Wallace

The singer collapsed on the stage, falling elegantly to the red velvet settee as her curled hair tumbled down her carefully arranged arms. The music swelled, and the haunting strum of violins rose over the harmony, leading the charge to the final note. The curtains fell, the dimmed lights brightened, and the noise of the audience replaced the orchestra.

A Gentleman in the box far above the general audience of the theatre sat back in his own red velvet chair, elbows on the armrest and hands clasped over his stomach. A pose of serenity, one might imagine him asleep, if not for his eyes. Deep brown eyes, their gaze undiminished by the glass of his spectacles as he looked over the edge of the box seat at the bustle of the people below. With his preference for a double-breasted suit and wire-rimmed glasses, he resembled the image of a grandfather looking lovingly over his children.

The curtains behind him rustled. Another man emerged, and he sat in the empty chair next to the Gentleman. The two could have been mistaken for the same age, but this man, with his partiality for slim cut suits,the latest technology, and his shrewd gaze, placed him as too young in people's minds for any sort of fatherhood. Perhaps a politician, or solicitor would come to mind, or maybe a Businessman. The older Gentleman spoke first, not taking his eyes off the audience.

What do you think of the opera?

I have to admit the set and costumes are well constructed, but I think the lead is a little pitchy, and her acting leaves something to be desired. And the story, well, it's as unbelievable as the acting.

You do not approve of any story with a happy ending

It's unrealistic. The hero's fall from favour, and then, by the pure goodness of their heart, they reap the reward at the end. Everything is tied up with a nice little bow. No, the real world is not so kind, and people are not so selfless.

Perhaps not every person, but that is what makes a hero – or heroine – worth immortalising. Take that woman down there, for example. I have seen her at the theatre, crying as tragedies play out, laughing at the comedies, and smiling with joy at the triumphs. You see she is not wealthy, and has no friends or partner to accompany her. But her empathy for the characters and the pleasure she takes in the theatre makes her far richer than any other. She could be a true heroine.

Would you bet on it?

The Gentleman shifted his gaze from the woman to the serpentine smile on his companion's face. The Businessman lifted an eyebrow; his taunting invitation to accept the challenge. The Gentleman sat up and carefully scrutinised the woman who had remained in her seat, her gaze on the closed curtains. He nodded.

I would. Same stakes as last time?

Of course. Shall we say a year? You'll see that even she can't remain unscathed from the tragedies of living.

A year, to this exact date. How will you prove it?

Three tests that we mutually judge.

Agreed, but you must not physically harm her.

Very well.

Will you stay for the second act?

Not if I want to keep my sanity.

***

The woman in question was Josephine. Hearing the announced intermission, she knew that the spell of the theatre had been broken. Other audience members began squeezing past her, glaring when she didn't shift her legs as they raced off, trying to get to the restroom before the line curved out the door. Josephine continued to stare at the heavy curtains, eyes watery, a handkerchief clutched in her hand, her mouth slightly parted. Slowly, she brought the handkerchief up to her eyes, dabbing the welled tears as she called forth the despair of the character, keeping it at the forefront of her mind until the curtains rose again. The movement jostled the program that balanced on her silk-clad leg, and it fell. She swiftly dipped to pick it up.

She saved each program, every ticket, even the newspaper reviews of the shows she attended. She couldn't afford to go to the theatre as often as she liked, but she'd been a true admirer of the stage ever since her father took her as a young girl. The performers were her idols and the composers her gods.

'All the unjustness we see in this broken world gets righted in the theatre.' Her father would say. But looking at her dressed in her Sunday best, he would quickly add, 'though that is no reason not to remain kind and hopeful, because sometimes, sometimes these tales come true.'

The clear night sky had turned dark and thunderous by the time the opera ended. The lead singer had been rescued from poverty and certain death by the rich young man who promptly married her. Josephine's palms still smarted from her rapid applause as she stepped out of the theatre's glow. Seeing the fat drops of rain, she jostled open her umbrella, only to find a half circle and two bent spokes. Awkwardly, she positioned it to shelter her as much as she could from the worst of the early spring downpour, but the wind picked up, beating the rain against her. It quickly plastered her dress to her legs and soaked through her stockings, making her shoes chafe against her heels as she limped to the bus stop.

As she continued fighting the wind, a body slammed into her. She fell, and a hand violently tugged the strap on her arm.

'My purse!' She yelled, looking for anyone who could help. But the bus stop was empty.

She felt the filth from the street sticking to her wet clothes. Her keys, her phone, everything she needed was in her purse. She pushed herself up, stumbled awkwardly while she forced down the tears. Just deal with one thing at a time, and when she was back in her warm flat, she could have a little cry over how disappointing the evening turned out.

After being told there was nothing they could do without any evidence, Josephine left the police station. Shivering, she hoped her neighbor was up and still had her spare key.

Just an unlucky day, she thought. *Tomorrow will be better.*

***

'Have I done something wrong?' Josephine looked around the room, disgusted with its peeling wallpaper that was stained yellow in the corners, the matted-down carpet of grimy brown, and the abstract art that resembled blood splatters. Now all common sights since she'd lost both her job and her flat.

It was the flat that went first – a leak upstairs made the roof fall in and flood everything. Her carefully curated small comforts were gone: the porcelain figures she'd collected from charity shops, her grandmother's needlepoint cushion, and the rug that sat beside her bed. Every morning she curled her feet into its plush tufts, steeling herself for the day. All of it was lost.

She managed to save some clothes; a couple suitcases worth, hauled to various hotel rooms. At first a temporary endeavour, until the landlord told her not to bother waiting. The clean hotel suites eventually turned to dingy motel rooms as her savings slowly trickled away. Savings she had to live on since she was let go from her job – redundancy was the excuse.

Josephine tried appealing to HR; she'd received no warnings, nor any indication that her job was on the chopping block. But her boss, usually a decent and affable man, was sharp – almost cruel – as he delivered her sentence: *she wasn't as productive as before, they needed to cut costs, and would she like to leave calmly, or would they need to call security?*

In shock, Josephine had nodded meekly, her head down as she packed up her things, her now-former coworkers avoiding her gaze. Cheeks flushed with shame, she realized that the friendly smiles and jokes in the break room had been nothing more than polite exchanges. She said no goodbyes when she left.

Today had been another fruitless day of handing out resumes, applying for any position advertised on job sites, and going into every place with a 'help wanted' sign. The motel room was an extra kick in the side when she returned. Her feet hurt, and the broken air conditioning locked the summer heat in the airless room. With no job leads and no landlord willing to take in an unemployed tennant, Josephine reasoned that she must have done something wrong to deserve this bad luck.

Her phone rang as she collapsed on the bed. Her heart thumped – perhaps it was someone *finally* calling her back.

'Hello?'

'Hi Josie,' a familiar voice said. Her friend Ellie, whose place had been 'too small to crash at,' when Josephine reached out.

'How are you?' Josephine asked.

'I'm fine, but there's something that's come up I need help with.' There was a pause. Josephine wondered if Ellie remembered refusing her.

'You remember Monty,' Ellie finally said. 'Well, he just had an appointment at the vet, and it looks like he needs surgery. I'm a bit behind on funds...I was wondering, if perhaps, if it's possible, maybe I could borrow some money?'

Some part of Josephine thought about placing a caveat in exchange for a place to stay. For help getting a job. But then she thought of how much her friend loved Monty, and her tearful confession that he was the only reason she made it through difficult times. Josephine had seen Ellie take in the shelter dog, and how he'd become a steadfast companion through her lousy exes and a cheating fiancée. And Josephine still had some savings. She simply told Ellie to pay her back when Monty recovered.

***

Two men stood on the cracked sidewalk, their skin an unearthly colour in the pale blue glow of the motel sign. They observed the drawn curtain of room 42B. The Gentleman turned to his companion.

See, in spite of her situation, her heart is open to others without expectation of reward.

All this proves is that she's an idiot. It's much too early to tell. She still has a roof over her head, food on her plate, and a family who loves her.

We shall see. You have two more tests. Perhaps you should not make it hinge on dying dogs. No one likes when the dog dies.

***

Josephine stepped out of the building, shoulders tense as the neon graffiti and barred windows loomed around her. Her backpack dug into her shoulders; everything she had left was shoved into its zipped pockets. It made quite a lumpy pillow, but it was less likely someone would steal it this way, a hard lesson she had learned on the first night when she'd lost her suitcase.

Her friends were gone too, perhaps scared of being associated with someone whose misfortune might rub off on them. They'd mysteriously gone silent after she'd withdrawn everything she had, and maxed out her credit card. There were likely notices piling up at her old address that the companies still had on record. Desperate, she had knocked on all her friend's doors, begging for a couch to crash on – just until she could get back on her feet. No one had answered.

Her phone rang, and her mother's image popped up on the screen. Josephine sighed – she'd already felt guilty that she had to tell her that she couldn't help them out with bills anymore. The first night at the shelter, she'd told herself it was only for the night, but by the second evening, she began trying to figure out how to ask her parents for money for a bus ticket home. At least they had a couch.

But it made her feel guilty to ask. They were retired, and had a very limited income with her father's medical bills. She caved after a month of sleeping with one eye open and hunger gnawing at her stomach.

'We can't right now, but we will start putting some money aside. We'll ask some folks at church if they can help out. Just hold on a little longer,' her mother had said, and Josephine could almost see the worried lines littering her mother's forehead.

Just a little longer. She imagined going down to the bus depot and asking for a ticket on the next bus. Then, an eight hour trip through the endless fields that seven years prior she had driven through with her father. The trunk of the car had been packed with suitcases and cards from friends wishing her well.

Their wishes might have faded, but her father would still be there to hug her when she arrived. She'd stutter out apologies for being a failure, but he would tell her it was all ok.

'Hey Mom,' she answered.

'It's your dad.'

The sidewalk dropped out from under Josephine's feet, and she grasped the rough brick wall next to her.

'What?'

'Your dad, he's on life support. They say it was – it was a heart attack. Just please, please get here. We need you.'

Her throat swelled, and every affirmative answer, every yes, every promise that she would be there as fast as possible, got stuck. Only the truth spewed out, tumbling over her thick and clumsy tongue

'I...I don't...I can't.'

'Please, he can't hold on for much longer.' Her mother's tears reached Josephine over the miles, heard through the tiny speaker.

'I'll try, I promise. I'll try.' The line went silent. A click followed. Josephine closed her eyes and leaned against the wall.

***

The two men sat on the bench in the park, autumn leaves swirling around their feet, avoiding the expensive leather. The Gentleman tapped his hand on his cane.

So, where is this test? Surely these desperate calls to friends and pitiful attempts at getting cash from strangers is not it.

Oh it's the build up, the tension. Don't you feel her desperation? A dying father, a scared mother, an unknown deadline looming closer and closer? The Businessman, forgoing his suit coat despite the weather, had draped his arms over the bench, taking up most of the space.

It is rather dramatic. You do know how to stage the moment, even if you dislike theatre.

I never said I didn't like the theatre. It's just not realistic. But here – here will be something real. Look, now she thinks – you see it in her eyes – she will take the ring.

No, she glanced at the ring, but she stares at the woman who dropped it. She understands losing something precious. Her empathy will win out.

This is taking too long. I'll give her a little nudge.

'Wait,' Josephine yelled, swooping to pick up the ring and run after the other lady.

The Gentleman threw his head back and laughed.

Maybe you would not be good at theatre. It seems your actors cannot follow your script.

The Businessman frowned.

Perhaps she doesn't care about her father enough.

The words of a sore loser.

Not yet. There's one more test.

I look forward to being just as thoroughly entertained.

***

The men left. They didn't stay to watch Josephine on the phone, tears streaming down her face as she tried to convince herself that she did the right thing. How she'd hoped that the lady would have given her a reward instead of a look of disdain, as though she were a thief no matter her integrity. And her father would be happy to know that she was good and righteous, even if she wasn't at his side.

But her mother's voice had been empty as she stated, 'I guess you won't be at the funeral either.'

Remembering her words made Josephine wish she had ripped the ring off the lady's finger before it had a chance to fall. If the two men had known her thoughts, they might have judged differently.

***

Once again, the Gentleman was in his reserved box. The woman was not there, of course. As he looked down upon the masses, he realized – perhaps part of him missed seeing her. That her presence, her reactions, made the performance all the more richer. The Businessman sat next to him, hands steepled under his chin in thought. He lowered them and finally voiced what was consuming his attention, for his thoughts were certainly not on the stage.

I've given it some thought. Yes, despite the loss of money and comfort, friends, and even her family – this woman still has not truly fallen. You see, it must be a matter of life and death. Only when she fears the possibility of death can we know her true nature.

You promised not to harm her.

It's the only way to make this a fair wager.

The Gentleman turned to the stage; the only violence adorning it was one of red scarves and pantomimed knives. Once the music faded, the actor would emerge whole, ready to take their bow. *Very well.* The Gentleman replied. *As long as she remains alive.*

Human lives are so fragile, but I'll do my best.

The Businessman rose and parted the curtain, allowing the Gentleman to finish the performance in peace. But the empty chair beside the Gentleman irritated him, just as much as the audience's loud yawns and muffled comments to their companions. The Gentleman left before the aria was even over.

***

Josephine stood on the corner of the busy street, hunched shoulders and a tired body that couldn't even muster the energy to shiver anymore. She felt as battered as the poor trees bending over in the winter wind, never given a chance to straighten. Each gust only pushed them further and further down until their branches slammed into the mud.

Her phone was a dead weight in her pocket. Dead, its charger lost, and useless anyways with all the unpaid bills. It didn't matter anymore. No matter how many times she tried calling, her mother refused to pick up.

Still, Josephine dreamed. She dreamed of her father's tales. How the good were rewarded, and the evil always justly condemned. It was the one thing she had to hold onto.

A child stood on the other side of the street. Her appearance was almost like magic, for she came out of nowhere. Josephine barely had time to register her before the child ran out in the street, hands outreached, chasing after a wind-caught ribbon. Pink, like her coat. Pigtails streaming behind her.

A horn blared.

Josephine didn't pause or stop to consider the risk to her own life.

The truck screeched. The pink ribbon landed next to the little girl with scraped palms. Josephine's body lay in the street.

Before the pain forced her eyes to close, she noticed two pairs of shoes beside her. A slightly worn, but shined brown leather oxford. The other had a mirror black finish and a pointed toe. Perhaps she dreamed of the conversation that ensued:

Well, I would say that was a decided outcome.

Hmmf, she just happens to be an outlier.

They do not write those shows for nothing. People like to hope for the fairness of the world.

It's all propaganda to appease the masses. Keep them in line.

You are just annoyed you lost.

Next time Father, we'll see.

Perhaps, but I do not make bets I will lose.

Well, aren't you coming?

Just a minute, she has been a good little prima donna after all.

And Josephine felt a soft caress in her hair as everything turned dark.

***

The timbre of the violins swelled, overtaking the accompanying instruments in the spring air while the curtains brushed in from the open balcony door to where the woman waited for her cue.

Her heart hammered as she listened to the murmurs of the crowd beneath the music.

'Are you ready honey?' Her mother touched her arm.

'Yes, I just need a few moments.'

'Alright,' her mother cracked open the door, then paused. 'Your dad would be so proud.'

Josephine nodded with a smile, then lifted her head to keep the tears from falling after her mother left. It had been a rough path to reconciliation. But her mother knew now how truly dire the situation had been. Theodore had helped.

He'd been by her bedside when she awoke. The nurses told her that he had been the one to call the ambulance and had covered all her hospital bills. He'd visited day after day, seeing her through the pain of healing her battered body and her struggle as she regained the ability to walk. Naturally, it wasn't long before they fell in love. And after he'd proposed, he'd encouraged her to reach out to her mother again. To think, a year ago she thought she would die on the streets.

'I do love weddings.'

Josephine started, turning to face the man who now stood behind her. She didn't recognize him, but Theodore had a lot of relatives. His old fashioned brown wool suit made her think he was an older family member. Perhaps a great uncle.

'I'm sorry, who are you?'

'Just a patron of the arts, and my dear, you performed beautifully.'

She gave him a small smile and gently said, 'I'm not an actor, perhaps you have confused me with someone else.'

'Ah, you think I am spouting nonsense, but no bother. I have come to say I appreciate your role in winning this bet. I must admit, I did think you might have broken and stolen that ring when your father died.'

'How did you know about that? Who are you?' Josephine looked at the door, firmly closed. She had never heard it open.

'I was always rooting for you my dear, and did I not give you a just reward? Your fiancée is very handsome, no? A house with a large garden, a place by the window you can curl up, and children on the way.' The Gentleman nodded to her midsection. Something she had only started to suspect herself.

She looked him up and down, taking notice of his shoes. A slightly worn, but well-cared for pair of oxfords.

But that conversation she heard had just been a hallucination! It had to have been a hallucination. If it was real—.

'No,' she muttered, shaking her head. 'No, no, no, no.' It wasn't possible. But neither did it seem probable that all of her misfortunes had piled up so neatly until she was left destitute. And that girl with the pink coat, it was like she had just appeared.

All those moments she had questioned what she had done to deserve this, and it was all for a bet. She let out a strangled sob and then screamed. The violins cut out, and voices clamoured as footsteps raced up the stairs, only to find the distraught bride.

The Businessman stood on the street. The Gentleman joined him and adjusted his spectacles as another scream made them both look back at the estate.

Well, I guess the wedding is delayed. She might even call off the whole thing. So, old man, it seems like you just proved me right. She sure as hell isn't happy with her ending. Probably doesn't feel it is justly deserved. Thing is, I didn't expect you to be this cruel. Allowing me to ruin her life is one thing, but telling her about it? And all just for a chance to gloat. Characters aren't meant to know how the author writes their story.

The Gentleman brushed the lint off his jacket, astutely ignoring the chaos in the distance.

It does not change the fact that I won. The bet was a year and three tests. You failed.

But this is so much better than winning. Let's play again sometime, old man. Next time I'll take a page out of your good book.

Love Bite

Lis Maestrelo

The muffled sound invades her ears beat by beat, pulling her out of heavy dreams. There's a hint of cheap soap and a blur of light overhead, but her eyes resist, not wanting to leave the comforting darkness.

Beat by beat, music.

The rave.

She is still here.

This realization lights up the shadows in her mind. At once she is back, wide awake.

On the floor, crumpled up beside the toilet, legs and arms let loose, head crooked with its own weight, she resembles a rag doll poorly arranged for a tea party. She raises her head slowly. Headache. It pulses with the rhythm of the strangling song that plays outside.

The drink. That unusual bitter taste was followed by dizziness, and his unsolicited hands all over her.

Then what?

Blackout.

She doesn't want to remember, doesn't want to wander into that dark room in her mind, find the little chain hanging from the light bulb and pull it, only to see her body being violated.

Nausea bubbles up from her stomach. Bile-flavored despair, guilt, shame...leaning over the toilet, she throws up.

But no. There's no other pain. Just a headache.

A flash of uncertain memories. She had lost him in the crowd, and escaped into the bathroom. She reaches and checks – yes, the stall is locked.

She is cornered, though. A rat in a box with holes. Soon a threatening eye could spy into the cubicle from above or below, or through the slits in the door frame. Is he out there waiting for her rodent head to poke out? A thin wooden door and chipped metal bolt offer little protection.

She listens, every sound emphasized: the irregular beats of her rapid heart, the buzz of a flickering light, a dripping faucet. But movement? None. Up on shaky legs, she opens the door a crack and peeks outside. No one there.

With an eroding emptiness in her stomach, she leaves the stall craving water. Craving for the cold liquid to rain down her palms, fill her mouth and wash away the sourness. The sink is dirty, too small, and it has a short faucet. Washing without touching the bowl is impossible. She splashes water on her face and checks her neck. The mark burns faintly.

Her solitary figure in the smudgy mirror. Artificial, like the fluorescent light above – high heels, short black dress, dark eye-makeup – a girl wearing the skin of someone she once was. A bitter smile cuts her face. Coming tonight was a desperate attempt to fit in, to be social again. But being close to people is a risk. Something can always get out of control. She could harm someone. No, she is not a monster. But if others were to know, that's how she would be seen. People fear what they can't understand...or control.

'Don't even shake his hand. I heard you can get it through sweat!' Her grandmother's voice is in her head, screeching some nonsense about their neighbor, a guy about her age – so young – who also tested positive in the test everyone wants to fail.

When she first got the Soul Tormenting Disease, she believed in all the urban legends too. Life was over. She wouldn't be able to look at herself in the mirror, or see daylight anymore, or sleep, or eat or breathe. In the months that followed, she refused to let her picture be taken, afraid it would show her true nature.

But she kept on living like everyone else, only with the extra burden of keeping it under control. Having a reckless heart, being too quick to trust – it had its consequences.

'You will change so much, Lucy,' Demetrius had said. He failed to mention that the changes would last forever, but the love was temporary. He left no note, only side effects.

She searches her purse for the blister pack – dark pills filled with chemicals that prevent her body from turning against herself. Usually kept well hidden, to avoid the taboo. Bubble gum, old receipts, wallet, her keys with the severed cartoon-bunny head hanging from the chain, but no sign of the meds. She glances at her phone. 11:10 – s*hit!*

How long had she been unconscious? She needs her dose. Soon.

Lucy, Lucy, what that heck are you doing?

Being reckless, being *this* reckless, was a symptom of loneliness. You become lonely when you try to hide parts of yourself.

Now she just wants to be home, back in her cramped room, reaching for the pills in the nightstand.

Where are you? She texts Mina.

Deep breath. Lucy opens the bathroom door and jumps into the chaos of the club. In the dark, she swims against the dancing crowd under the frenetic light show. EXIT glows ahead, each letter burning in faint neon green. Now and then she looks over her shoulder as she pushes through the writhing bodies that resist and ignore her, dragging her back.

A cold hand grabs her by the arm. Her heart stops. But it's only Adelia, with her crazy nails and wild hair.

'Are you going?' Adelia shouts. 'Did you see Mina?' Lucy asks. 'What?'

Damn. Too loud. The pulsing electronic beats muffle every

word, so she tries to speak slower, louder.

'Where. Is. Mina?' 'Oh yeah!' Adelia smiles and nods. 'I'm having fun too!'

And she resumes her dance, spilling some of her drink out of her plastic cup.

Forget it. Under the alternating shadows and lights, Lucy wedges her way out through the ocean of moving human parts. With each step, the walls close in, the crowd tightens. Sensing the weight of eyes upon her, she glances behind. Just her imagination, right? Yet, a shiver runs up her spine.

Soon she is at the staircase that leads out, where a sign on the ceiling reads *Poem Reading Fridays 1AM* and the walls are covered with posters of the gigs to come. Twelve steps, and at last the embrace of the fresh night air.

A message arrives from Mina. *Hey, I'm with Marcus at his place.*

She just freaking *left*? Lucy leans against the brick wall. A nearby group of smokers glances over.

You were supposed to be my ride, freakhead. Thanks for being so reliable. She taps into her phone.

Come on, you seemed to be having fun with that guy.

Christ Mina! He spiked my drink.

No answer back.

11:20, her phone says. Only half an hour to make it to the station and get the last train. Alone. But the mark burns stronger, and there's no time left to consider alternative plans.

Enveloped in a coat that doesn't warm her up, Lucy rushes through the empty streets, high heels clacking against the concrete. The cold wind blows on her bare legs, violating the gap in her dress.

Two blocks on, she knows she's not alone.

Footsteps echo from behind. She doesn't turn around. Doesn't dare. There's a strange feeling of needle-pricking on the tips of her fingers; she must be careful now, or her hands will act as if they don't belong to her anymore.

She walks a little faster, and soon she's almost running. Faded windows and closed roll-up metal doors offer no help. He whistles, snaps his fingers, toying with her. She glances behind – a mistake that makes her fall. With a stinging knee she rises, forcing her shaky legs to keep going. She rushes into the tunnel, the throat of a long concrete snake that leads to the train station. If she can keep it together just a little longer, she will be home, have her dose, and be herself again, no harm done. But the burning on her neck intensifies, spreading through her entire body. She halts.

Shadows fall over her eyes, and sound fills her ears. A blind symphony of chaos, of pain, of confusing lines that dance in her mind's darkness. Acutely intensifying. Calming down. Subsiding to a melody of echoes, drawing forms she can't make out nor understand. Behind her, she hears waves of noise, steps reverberating on the curved tunnel walls.

He's close. Too close. *Pulse, pulse, pulse*, in his veins. Wasn't drugging her enough? No, he wants her soul. How clever he must feel. Empty tunnel, lonely girl.

The paralyzing pain takes over her body. Her legs won't obey, for the delicious warm scent fills her nostrils, and she can't help it now. That thirst, the one she fears, the one she hates, crawls up from a place deep inside her.

Her teeth elongate. When she turns around with glowing-red eyes, he stops, and his little smirk of victory disappears.

As he runs, the staccato rhythm of his heart increases the smell of blood, and her mind gives in completely to the curse.

'Don't worry,' Demetrius had said long ago. 'It won't hurt. It'll only leave a small mark, a love bite.'

Not this time. Not for this stranger.

Her teeth pierce deep into the warm flesh. The scream of a predator becoming prey flies with the wind, dies in the night.

She makes sure to suck him dry. Until he's nothing but a corpse. A dead man with a disfigured mockery of a kiss on his neck.

A Volunteer Calls

Fiona Black

I'm an out of work actress with nowhere to act,
and present my skills at the home for 'female delinquents'.
I am met by the COOK and shown in.
On the floor of the lounge are four teens,
PRINCESS, who carries a knife, asks 'What do you want?'
'To offer my help,' I reply. She says she's OK her Dad'll
fetch her one day. I suggest that we put on a play.

JEWEL wants to know if I have a man,
I say, 'Yes,'
and 'How many kids?'
I say, 'None.'
'You're a fool. A man and no kids – what if he goes?
With kids you get money for life.'
Jewel, 16, explains, 'I have three,
I'm getting a place in that new block of flats
once I've learnt to make toast and potatoes and peas.'

SCARLETT sees her weans once a month
which is more than enough. CHANEL doesn't speak
but opens a window, leans out for a smoke.
Scarlett's sussed, gets money
from men she sees on the sly but is worried for me.
I say I'm OK,
I'm not the one needing help.

Princess remembers a play at her school –
a girl dies drinking cheap bleach.They nod
having been there themselves. 'That's Priestley,'
I say, 'it's great it's about being rejected.'
Chanel screams that all she wants is a job,
she can copy down numbers, re-train
as a parking attendant – but the Council said no.
Jewel whispers, 'That's coz, she went mad
when her first baby died. Smashed up the hospital ward'
Chanel hears, grabs Jewel's hair – who howls,
Cook calls from the kitchen, 'Shut up or no tea.'
Chanel snarls but backs off, Princess says,
'We'll write you a script.' and sharpens her knife
to make us blood sisters.

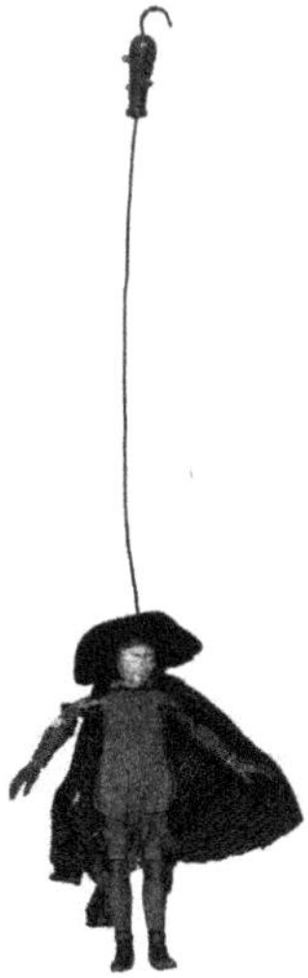

Act III

Is this a dagger which I see before me,
The handle toward my hand? Come, let me clutch thee.

Macbeth II • 1

Jakka's Dilemma

Rory MacCallum

She could smell out the lonely, and the Next Level nightdross bar drew plenty like them in.

Spacers from across the galaxy ended up here, looking for a little delight to ease their sorrows. Looking for whatever distraction their hard cash could buy. And this night, like most nights, Jakka cruised the tables and bar, seeking out that heady scent of desperation.

She drew heavily on her libre cigarette as she prowled, and the narcotic cast musky clouds about her as she exhaled the smoke, feeling the benefit of its intoxicating kick. But she knew not to get too wasted. Not here in the bar. She was a professional, after all, and had money to make, both for herself and for her pimp who was likely lurking close by somewhere in the shadows.

'Feeling lonely, spacer?' She tried on one forlorn looking crewman sitting by himself at the bar. He appeared Lamorhian, going by his blue and gold-speckled skin colour. He was likely using Calaxus as a jump point for an interstellar journey.

'How much for… you know?' the man asked Jakka. She gave him her price.

He shook his head. 'That's too much.'

'Well, it doesn't have to be the full deal. There are…lighter options,' she said to the humanoid.

But the creature shook his head. 'Still too much. Leave me in peace,' he grumbled. Jakka took the hint. There were other desperate creatures in the bar, after all. And the night was still young; there was plenty of time for earning an easy – or not-so-easy – buck.

She drew again on the libre as she slinked away from the Lamohrian. More and more, she noticed lately, she needed the solace of the drug. She was getting on in years to still be caught up in this game, a fact she was all too vividly aware of. But she had a young daughter, responsibilities, and a not exactly dazzling skill-set with which to prosper on the vast space module that was Calaxus. So, she worked here at the nightdross bar, growing sadder with each passing night as she watched the horizon of her possibilities shrink ever smaller. If it wasn't for her daughter, she didn't know what she would do; what reason she would have to get out of bed each day.

She saw another potential customer and plastered on a smile. This one looked a bit more responsive, going by the idiot grin he was directing her way. Well, going by the grin and the plethora of empty beer bottles dotted about his table. Jakka grinned to herself and moved in for the kill. She knew easy prey when she saw it. Oh yes, she knew it all too well.

'Want to come round the back with me, spacer?' she asked the drunk man. He was big – looked human, a species not too far removed in appearance from her own kind. He reached out a thick arm and drew her in easily to sit on his lap.

'Now, what would I like to do with you, my pretty?' he said, slurring his words while looking down her low-cut neckline.

'Well, if you come with me, you can show me,' Jakka teased.

The big, beaming spacer nodded. 'Yeah, I think I'd like that.' They moved through the dark, smoky environment of the Next Level, ready to consummate the transaction.

It went easily enough, Jakka was relieved to discover. The spacer's needs were distinctly vanilla, and there were no complicated requests, an occasional hazard about her work which she detested. He left her with no violence and the merest hint of disdain. A good result, as far as she was concerned.

***

It was getting into the tenth hour when *he* appeared. He was dressed like a spacer and ordered a beer at the bar before sitting at a corner table to brood in the shadows in peace, away from the hullabaloo.

Jakka noticed him immediatly. He appeared to be human, but there was something about him. He kept casting wary glances around him, and at the front entrance of the Next Level in particular. A little unsure of herself, Jakka let some time pass before she made her move.

'Hard for a spacer to be here alone,' she said, sidling up to the man. Like with every new customer, Jakka assessed the situation: was he a psycho? Was he dangerous? Would he pay up with good grace? But then she caught a look in his eyes and was surprised: she could swear she caught the glow of kindness.

He looked up from his table with a smile. 'Sorry, missy. I'm not in the market.'

She felt something move within her: something nameless and ineffable which she could not pin down. Dread, perhaps. Or perhaps something that felt weirdly close to love. Whatever it was, it gave her courage, and she would not be dissuaded by this stranger so easily.

'You look lonely. A little cash can buy my time, you know,' she said. 'I could sit, and we could talk.'

'I don't have much to talk about,' the spacer said.

'I'm sure that's not true. You could tell me about your adventures,' she persisted.

But he just smiled. 'Uh-uh. 'Fraid not. No adventures to talk of either.'

'What's your name, stranger?' Jakka asked. She could see him more clearly now as her eyes had adjusted to the shadows of the corner. He wasn't exactly a youth – she estimated that he was in his mid to late thirties. His looks weren't without a certain charm, despite his savagely shorn head. She would be disgruntled, frankly, to let this one pass.

'Treadway,' the man answered.

'I'm Jakka, Treadway,' she said. 'Maybe you would at least like to buy me a drink?'

Something in Treadway seemed to relent. *Maybe*, she thought, *he wanted company after all. Or maybe*, she realised, *he just wanted to get information*. A sudden disquiet was aroused in her at this thought.

'Okay,' the man said, suddenly seeming indulgent. 'What will it be?'

'Draava juice,' Jakka said, the usual drink she allowed customers to buy her, if they were feeling generous. It was only mildly alcoholic and wouldn't befuddle her faculties too much.

'One Draava juice coming right up,' Treadway said, getting up to go to the bar.

While he was at the bar, Jakka's pimp, Grazer, came to her with his mouth turned down in the type of frown he wore when he lost a bet.

'Keep the spacer talking. I've just had word, he's of interest to the Dreaming. Sentinels are on their way as we speak.' With a sneer and a grumble, Grazer quickly departed, subsumed by the shadows.

Jakka felt a sudden terror. Dealings with the Dreaming, the governing agency of Calaxus, always meant no good. And she liked this spacer; she didn't want to betray him. But she knew better than to cross the Dreaming. And she knew better than to question the orders of her pimp. So, when Treadway returned with the drinks, she plastered her smile on again, and showered him with her benevolence.

'You're not a regular,' Jakka noted after he sat down.

'Nah. I'm just passing through.'

'And what brings you to Calaxus, hmm?'

The man seemed wary of this particular question. 'Do I need a reason?'.

Jakka spoke quickly to recover the situation. 'Not at all. Not at all,' she said. 'You're just a spacer with a notion, eh?' She exhaled some more libre smoke, in an attempt to cover up her nervousness, before beaming at Treadway again.

'That's right,' he said. 'I'm just a spacer with a notion. Nothing else.'

They chatted some more about this and that, none of it of much consequence. But she couldn't help noticing that Treadway's eyes were never far from the entrance. It was almost as if he were expecting trouble.

'What makes you so jumpy?' she eventually asked.

'We deep spacers aren't used to crowds. So many people in one place makes me kind of…restless.'

'But I'm here, sweetie. And my offer still stands. I'll even give you a discount, on account of your…charms,' she said with a grin.

Treadway shook his head again. 'I'm really not interested. In need of a top up?' he asked, nodding to her empty glass.

'Sure,' she said. 'I just need to powder my nose first.'

Jakka got up and walked away, as if heading to the latrine, but really, she wanted a word with Grazer, to find out why this very inoffensive specimen could be of possible interest to the Dreaming. After all, she was losing hours of her time that she could be selling. In the shadows, she saw him, lurking. Grazer was always lurking close by.

'He seems a total innocent,' she said to him. 'Why does the Dreaming want him?'

'That's not our concern,' Grazer replied.

He was right, of course, Jakka knew. Too much curiosity in the Dreaming was as likely to shorten one's life as displaying an over-zealous amount of idealism. But, still, she persisted, despite the danger. Her curiosity piqued, she had to know.

'What is he? Pirate? Smuggler? Trafficker?' she asked.

The man sighed. 'All right. Since it's your head on the line. Apparently, he's White Rose.'

'You mean, he's with the *insurgency*?'

Grazer nodded. 'He's a rebel. And you know how much the Dreaming hates rebels.'

A new fear took hold of her. If the Dreaming apprehended Treadway, it would almost certainly lead to his death. Once they had wrung all the information out of him that they could, they would dispose of him as ruthlessly as they did everything else in their dominion of the stars. The White Rose, after all, was number one in their list of outlawed affiliations.

Still, she couldn't help but feel admiration for the spacer. To do what he did took guts. To serve the White Rose was no idle commitment. Reluctant, Jakka returned to her seat and took up her drink with all the good grace she could muster.

'Cheers,' she said to the White Rose man, trying to smile.

'Cheers,' came the reply but, she noticed, Treadway's eyes wandered back to the Next Level's point of access. He was clearly on the lookout. They chatted some more, and Jakka summoned all her acting skills to appear blithely unconcerned. Tried not to come over as anxious or stilted. She knew her role here: to keep Treadway talking till the Sentinels' trap was sprung. But she didn't want to play into that role, she didn't want to be part of the system.

She wondered, *how could she warn him without suspicion falling on herself?* She knew if he bolted before the Sentinels got here, they would blame the failure of their mission on her. She would make a convenient scapegoat when they explained their failure to their superiors.

And yet Jakka thought: *what was her life when balanced with the cause of Treadway and the White Rose in general?* If she had grown up in a world the White Rose envisioned, she wouldn't have to wander Next Level each night hoping for enough money to make rent. And her daughter, she would have a better future. Yes, she had no reason to love the Dreaming, but if it wasn't for her daughter, Leona...

She would do what, exactly?

She took a long draw on her libre cigarette in an attempt to calm her nerves. Treadway, sitting across the table, looked relatively at ease, almost as if he were enjoying himself.

It was enough to break her heart.

If she was absent, well...Jakka's own mother would step in to raise the child. Would probably do a better job of it, too. *After all,* she reproved herself unsparingly, *what kind of upbringing was it to give your child while you earned your living the way Jakka earned hers? What kind of future was she creating for her precious Leona?*

She glanced nervously towards the door, waiting for the dreaded appearance of the Sentinels. *Couldn't be far away now,* she realised. A sudden rage at the injustice of her predicament tore its way through her breast. *Why had the universe put her in this bloody quandary?* All she had ever wanted was to stay clear of trouble and find a little love in her life.

'You seem a little jumpy.' Treadway must have noticed her anxiety.

Jakka smiled. 'Working in a nightdross bar can do that to a girl. You meet all sorts.' In the future, she would be amazed at the courage it took. But it would also give her great pride as she remembered uttering the three words: 'Even White Rose.' She gave Treadway a long, even look, the better to convey her assuredness.

Treadway looked at her for some long moments. His eyes dropped to look at his glass on the table, then he met her gaze once more. 'How did you know?'

'Never mind that now,' she said. 'You've got to get out of here. Sentinels are coming.'

The White Rose man seemed suddenly more focused and alert. His eyes sparked as if he was once again recalling the atrocities the Dreaming presided over in the name of their galactic order. And the knowledge of the precariousness of his own situation was evident by the expression on his face, Jakka saw.

'Then I have to get out of here,' he rose to leave.

Jakka shook her head. 'Not that way,' she nodded towards the front entrance. 'They could be right outside.'

Treadway turned back towards her. 'Then what do you suggest?'

'There's a back exit,' Jakka said. 'It's down the corridor, a bit to the left of the latrines. Follow the corridor to the fire exit and it takes you to an alley. Left from the alley is a pod station, no more than twenty metres away. Get on the first available pod and you'll be on the other side of Calaxus in no time, lost in the crowds and lost to the Dreaming. For now.'

A welter of emotions was evident on his face. Jakka could see that he was calculating whether he could trust her. But, surely he must realise that he had no choice.

'You do realise you're risking your life?' Treadway asked.

Jakka nodded.

'I wish I could thank you.'

'Just do whatever you came here to do. That will be thanks enough.'

Treadway held her gaze for what seemed an eternity. Then, with the briefest nod of thanks, he was lost in the crowd, on his way to the back exit.

Jakka took a final long drag of her libre cigarette, then stubbed it out in the ashtray. She sat at the table for some minutes, feeling the gaze of Grazer burn its way into her flesh. And soon four Sentinels appeared at the front entrance of the Next Level. She took a sip of her Draava juice, and sat with as much calm and poise as she could muster. She knew the Sentinels were no longer here to apprehend Treadway. News of his escape would have certainly reached them. They had come for different quarry. Undoubtedly, they had come for herself. She gave a small smile, and lifted her glass in cheers towards the empty seat across from her.

To Leona, to a better future, and to no more bloody Dreaming.

The Dinner Party

Charlie Hilton

A night of tedious predictability. One liners fall
flatter than the souffle, anecdotes and steak tough
as leather, segues into conversation forced
like the general bonhomie of this tired affair.
But the evening takes a turn when I find myself

across from you, a mutual joy in rolling eyes
at sloppy jokes and talking points like well-worn
b-list movie scripts, us the extras murmuring
rhubarb, rhubarb, rhubarb, the camera keeps us
soft and out of focus, where no one else can see

your flashing smile, when you talk to me of Chekov
and the gun you keep concealed in your clutch.
The room is dead to us as we laugh across dessert –
now it's only you and me, the moonlight shining
in your eyes, fingers wrapped around your wine glass.

White Picket Smiles

C. H. Lei

Her Then

As far as you can remember, Lacey Schumacher always smelled like shit.

She didn't shower or bathe. Her matted hair and wild eyes gave her the look of a feral cat, and her clothes sported more holes than a chain-link fence. It just so happened you two lived on the same street. Lacey needed a buddy, and that duty got shunted onto you. You didn't like her, so you tried doing what all good kids were taught: sharing her with your friends.

'She's a neighbor,' you said, a twinge of begging in your voice. Not to plead her case, but hoping they could pity you. 'It's just recess.'

The playground council wasn't convinced. Fifteen minutes was a long time in grade school. Ruin that, and the entire day could go wrong. Why bother weighing the positives and negatives when the jury's already decided?

'Why does she reek?' Danika asked, pinching her nose. Her other friends nodded in unison, deferring to her. 'Ew god, what's with her hair?'

You couldn't think of a defense. Danika already said the two-letter death sentence. Nobody recovers from that. Lacey was branded.

You pursed your lips, keeping them shut.

Seconds later, the final judgment, not just metered out to your neighbor, but to you as well: 'I don't want to be friends with you if you're friends with *her.*'

Simple as that.

One by one, they left you. Social suicide in the third grade. No more play dates, goodbye birthday party invites. Just you and Lacey Schumacher, or as she became known, that girl.

Ten minutes later, Lacey was still crying. She apologized, or at least you think she did, multiple times.

The shock of this great friendship schism would be delayed a couple days before a magnificent breakdown, but thankfully, you could adapt.

'Come on,' you tugged at her sleeve. Just the hem. With your fingernails. 'Let's bully the younger kids out of the sandbox and make a castle or something.'

Lacey didn't stir up trouble. She never acted out, didn't kiss you in ways she was not supposed to, and her arms stayed free from anything sharp. Lacey was Lacey. You two were inseparable for years, bonded with invisible zip ties.

And then CPS got called.

Nothing happened after the many check-ups and investigations, but still, Lacey's parents pulled her out of school. Practically from life.

You don't see her again for a long time.

***

Her Now

'Oh my god, it's been so long!'

It takes forever for you to remember your best friend's face.

You're walking home on break from college when she's on you. Long blonde hair, wide smile. She reeks with extroversion and popularity. Before you can defend yourself, you're accosted with squeals of exuberance in place of a knife. You instantly think you're being scammed, but not even Dustin Hoffman can act this giddy.

'I knew it was you when I saw you!' exclaims the stranger.

Your brows furrow. 'Um, excuse me, sorry, who are—?'

By the time you realize who it is, you're in her snare. She squeezes as if trying to pop your eyes from their sockets. 'Come on, you couldn't have forgotten *me*, right?'

When people *really* change during their teen years, it's almost always downhill the steep slope of weirdness. Piercings in atypical places, tattoos with provocative images, offensively dyed hair. Punk, goth, metal. Alternative styles. You took that plunge at sixteen, embraced it, never went back.

This is the first *Princess Diaries* glow-up you've ever seen in real life. You've imagined what Lacey might've looked like now, and probably will ashamedly later admit that you expected her with an addict's complexion or covered with maggots.

Her skin is pale and flawless. Fashion straight from California. Pastel colours, tight jeans, exposed stomach. Pierced navel. Bright blue eyes glimmer behind perched sunglasses. A major glow-up for sure, not just of her image, but her entire being.

You're caught up in her wave. Before you realize it, you're sitting on a park bench outside of an ice cream parlor, her treat.

You get your usual weirdness, purple yam with coconut shavings on a waffle cone. Lacey orders plain vanilla.

'I thought you hated those basic flavors,' you say. 'The girl that suicided every soda fountain drink going for vanilla? And not even the French one.'

'It's the most popular flavor for a reason,' Lacey points out. 'Like pop music is pop music because it's, well, popular.'

'Yeah, but it's basic. And just because something's popular doesn't make it good.'

'I also like chocolate. Sometimes I do cookies 'n cream if I'm feeling spicy.'

The ice cream goes away fast. Blame summer for that. A single scoop is not enough to weather the heat. But when – surprisingly – Lacey paid, you couldn't go overboard.

The catch up feels superficial. Sure, you ramble and rant about the positives and negatives of college. But, Lacey just allows you to speak, and answers with ambiguity, or not at all. You can't help thinking that she feels off somehow. It's nigh impossible to connect this person with the girl in your memories. Ten years is a long time, sure, but still.

'What happened to you, Lace?' you finally ask. 'You just disappeared. Gone. I tried knocking on your door. Nothing. I even snuck around the entire house one time, peering through windows.'

After a summer of persistence, your efforts were left forgotten as puberty took hold during the terror known as middle school. Stress and emotions and too many memories painted vivid shades of embarrassment. And the least said of high school, the better. Yes, passing Lacey's house was part of all commutes, but after a while, the building just blended in with all the others, for better or worse. Not even your mom mentioned her after a while.

Lacey turns to you, she's smiling.

Her teeth look like plastic.

'Hey, wanna come back to my place, for old time's sake?'

***

Her House Then

You've been inside Lacey's house just once before she disappeared, and only because you really, really, *really* needed to go. The first thing you remember is being thankful they didn't own any pets. Black trash bags, full and bulging, lay on the floor in piles. Too many plants sat on shelves and hung from the walls, their roots overgrown as if looking for escape.

It was a miracle that you remained unscathed in your rush.

The bathroom looked just as bad. Bottles littered the counter like tombstones in a Hong Kong cemetery. Clothes of varying degrees of cleanliness covered the tiles. It reeked of mold and bad perfume. Still, there was nothing you could do but just sit on the toilet and be vulnerable.

Not even five seconds of solitude in, *knock, knock, knock.*

'Um, occupied,' you called out.

'Hey.' Lacey's voice, muffled. 'Can I come in? I don't like being alone.'

At first you thought it was a technique to escape bullying when you needed to leave class. The tag-a-long, afraid of her own shadow. Then it started happening all over. Your place. Fast food restaurants. The movies. But her own house? Nothing scarier than being left to the wilderness beyond her own backyard. Those untouched woodlands were a place she always refused to go.

Before you could answer with an emphatic no, the door – that you forgot to lock – opened and Lacey rushed inside. She ignored you with your pants down, instead charging for the safety of the tub.

You finished your business, cringing at how monstrous the flush sounded.

Pulling the shower curtain back revealed your friend, her legs drawn up, eyes staring somewhere not there. Sometimes – most of the time – you wondered what you did to deserve this.

'Why can't you be normal?' you asked, and crawled into the other end of the bathtub at her behest. 'You know, the bathtub can be used for more things besides hiding.'

But Lacey wasn't with you. Whatever happened had terrified her.

And as far as you knew, her parents weren't home.

***

Her House Now

The inside is like a doll's house. Lacquered wood floors, walls painted white, the smell of air freshener. Growing up, you always marveled at how most other houses were cleaner than yours. Her place now makes your home feel like a pig sty.

'Shoes off,' Lacey orders, and you obey.

Not only is everything spotless, the place is almost barren now. It's like looking at photos from a real estate website – *For Sale: three bedroom, two bath* – with all the staging furniture included, the type that cohesively worked, but lacked style beyond being new.

Absent-minded, you reach for one of the potted plants and cringe as the artificial material rubs against your skin.

'Make yourself at home,' Lacey says. 'Mi casa and whatever.'

Honest to god, you try.

'This is the first time I've seen the floor here.' You've said worse to less-forgiving people. 'How long did it take you to clean this up?'

'Not as long as you might think,' Lacey says. Despite directing you in with an invisible lead, she's never taken her eyes off you.

When was the last time she blinked?

'Oh, well it's a heck of a renovation,' you say. 'Makes my place look cluttered as all hell now. Even when I left for college we were never fully unpacked from before.'

'Really?' A flicker of *something* passes over Lacey's face, but it's gone before you can process just what it was. 'I would think this is how a standard house is. Normal.'

There's something about empty houses and their lack of life. Even following Lacey inside, it feels like urban exploration without the ruins. Your mind instantly goes 'haunted' from the atmosphere alone.

It's in the stillness that you hear the sound. Feet, shoes – loud ones.

You two are not alone.

***

Her Parents Then

Lacey's parents were almost never around.

The few times you remember seeing them, the odor of cigarettes and beer clung to them like a koala to a tree.

They always looked tired.

Like they had given up.

***

Her Parents Now

'My dear, it's been so long!' Lacey's mom welcomes you into her embrace, though your arms are at your side. Her greeting is very European, the two not-kisses at the cheeks. 'I recognized you when I saw you!' Then to Lacey, 'You should have texted or called me that you were going to bring a friend over.'

'Sorry.' Lacey pretends to look apologetic. 'It was just so sudden. Like fate.'

They smile. Laugh.

Identical sounds coming from identical mouths.

Their teeth look like plastic.

You can accept puberty for Lacey. God knows all the stuff it has given you. Early too. Precocious. Enough to single you out in class. Your face. Your voice. Your height. Your—

You imagined Mrs. Schumacher taller. Could be because of your then-kid height. But everything else about her? There's a limit to what plastic surgery can do. She and Lacey look related, as mother and daughter should, yet it's all wrong.

It's when she starts talking about your past, the way you two played in the backyard among other familiar stories that lowers your guard. You don't remember the woman being around, but she paints the memories with such detail that she must've been there, right? 'Thank you for being friends with Lacey. We never did have a chance to say that.'

Upstairs, a series of thumps silences everyone below. Both Lacey and her mom's faces drop for a moment before they're jovial again. A momentary malfunction.

'The dog,' says Lacey's mom.

Lacey is less convincing. 'We have a big one, and she gets rowdy.'

For the first time in what feels like forever, she blinks.

'Yes, he does,' her mom adds.

Your brows furrow. 'But dogs are supposed to be—' *Not living just on the second floor.*

Two pairs of unblinking eyes shut you up. From above, *thump, thump, thump-thump, thump*. For a moment, you think you hear something crying out in decidedly not-canine-like noises.

Then, more noise. New noise. The sound of a door opening and closing. The thuds of heavy feet coming downstairs.

'I hope nobody's talking about me down there!' calls a sing-song voice, baritone-deep and lumbering.

The person that could only be Lacey's dad wears a maroon sweater. His gray hair recedes to the back of his skull, begging for a toupee. Circular spectacles sit on the edge of his nose.

Lacey practically squeals, and gives the man a kiss on the cheek. 'Hey, daddy!' she says loudly. 'Guess who it is? Come on, guess!'

Lacey's dad smiles.

His teeth look like plastic.

'You know, I knew it was you when I saw you!'

***

Lunch Then

You were a chubby kid, especially once the Human Twig became a constant annoyance in your life. As it turned out, Lacey was better than any fad diet, she just vacuumed up any donations you gave her. The school lunch program could never bring nutrition to a skeleton. Sharing your food felt like giving to charity, and you got to shed a few pounds as an added bonus.

'Here,' you said, handing her half of your sandwich. 'It's tuna salad today.'

Lacey took the offering without thanks. Instead, she mumbled, 'I hate fish,' and ripped out a sizable chunk with her teeth.

It was fun watching her eat, like an animal at a zoo. Everything you gave her always disappeared within seconds. Lack of nutrition rendered your friend a shrimp. She wore rags bought years ago, and they still fit. The cost of replacing your own wardrobe even in the first steps of puberty was nearing four digits.

'Catch.' You ripped off a bit of your half, and tossed it high into the air.

Lacey failed to catch it. Not once did she ever succeed. It would always hit the ground.

Not that it mattered. For Lacey, the five-second rule didn't exist.

***

Lunch Now

'I just work from home. Still do the good ol' nine to five. Nose to the grindstone, you know?'

Despite all the talk, you still don't know what Lacey's dad actually does. Business something. A foreign corporation. Maybe accounting? Marketing? Your pointed questions return nebulous answers.

The conversation fades once Lacey's mom returns from the kitchen with plates, and places them in front of everyone at the table.

Steaks. Honest to god steaks. Medium rare. They take up half of the entire plate. To the side of the slab of meat, mashed potatoes and salad.

They say grace – you don't remember if the Schumachers are religious; born again, maybe? – which is your cue to turn off your ears.

In the corner of the dining room, an analog clock. The hands read 1:15 P.M.

'Rather big meal for just lunch,' you say.

Lacey blinks. 'It's just an early dinner,' she justifies quickly, as if she knew they made a misstep. 'You know, it's just one of those family eccentricities!'

Then, as if prompted, they laugh. All three, open-mouthed, all eyes on you. Three copies of the same sound, pitch shifted for each member of the Schumacher family.

Again you hear sounds from upstairs. Scraping. Moaning?

The meat tastes weird.

Who or what is making that noise?

Why is everyone so weird?

They're still laughing.

Their teeth look like plastic.

***

Your Friendship Then

Lacey always sat in the back of the class, downwind from everybody else, away from their stares. Through guilt by association, you're stuck in the ass-end of the desks as well.

You tried everything over the years. New clothes, haircut, a bath, makeup, nail art. No matter what, Lacey's still weird. Nobody will talk to her. Or you still.

When you finally gave up, she's crying again, apologizing through snot-filled sniffles. You can't believe you're feeling bad for her. The loser has grown on you like kudzu overtaking a field.

'You know what?' you said, 'Forget them. You be you, I'll be me, and they'll be them. And who wants to be like them anyway?'

'I do,' Lacey sobbed.

***

Your Friendship Now.

You accept the goodbye hug, but keep your hands at your side. Before, Lacey read like a picture book. She's inscrutable now. Nobody ever smiles that much.

Now that you think about it, the color of her eyes are different than you remember.

Hazel. They were definitely hazel.

'Thanks for coming by,' she says. 'It means a lot to me – hey, we should exchange numbers. You free sometime tomorrow? Oh, remember Danika? We're like besties now. Though you're still my number one. We should have, like, a get together. How long are you going to be in town?'

Shorter than you intended, if it means seeing her around.

Not that you can say that out loud.

'Maybe like two weeks or so?'

Lacey takes your phone, infects your contacts. Her name is sandwiched between too many heart emojis. 'Hope you have an unlimited plan. I'm chatty.'

'I'll make sure to mute your texts then.'

She takes it as a joke – and thankfully doesn't laugh or show her teeth.

You have to pull yourself away, but freedom is ensured once you do. Home is only two blocks away. Far enough. A reassuring thought as you power walk away, Lacey waving you off.

Not even halfway to your house and you feel sick. Maybe it's something you ate, maybe having to suffer through your then-best friend and her off-putting parents.

Your phone buzzes with excitement as Lacey starts texting you. You look back. Her parents are now outside, hand over head. All three of their motions are in sync.

'God, she's so strange now,' you utter, a shiver tickling your spine. 'A family of weirdos.'

Two blocks is not far enough.

***

'I saw Lacey today,' you say during dinner. It's just you and your parents. They're the same as they've always been. It should not feel this reassuring. 'She's really changed.'

'She's a nice girl,' mom says. 'Works hard now, looks happier than she did before.'

'She invited me over to her house tomorrow,' you say, hoping they give you some excuse. You live so close, and for some reason, you don't want to see Lacey angry. 'She sent me fourteen texts until I said yes.'

'You should go,' dad says in Mandarin. 'Having proper friends would be good for you. Maybe they can save you from these tendencies that are ruining your life.'

Tendencies meaning your current buddies, your band; the art on your arms, back, and chest.

'I don't think I will,' you say. If they're not going to help you, you're going to make a stand. 'I'm not going to get rehabbed by hanging around the 'proper' folk. Besides, Lacey's...off. Her parents too. It's like they're trying too hard to be people. It's like, say, if Uncle Aaron started to only use chopsticks and started only listening to Peking opera.'

'I like Peking opera, there's nothing wrong with that,' dad retorts. 'They're just white people. They're always off with that white picket whatever.'

'No, you're missing the point, I—'

'You got nothing else to do, it wouldn't hurt.' Mom interrupts. 'Go and have fun. I'll make some snacks. It's been a while, after all.'

***

It's with great exertion that you ring the doorbell the next day. You can see Lacey behind the glass, standing behind the door as if waiting for your return. As if she's never moved from that very spot. Another embrace. She takes you by the hand and leads you inside.

'Everybody's already here,' she says. 'We've been talking up a storm. Disturbing the peace.'

The only sounds you hear are your feet on the polished wood floor.

You're dragged to the end of the hallway into the lounge, where the room explodes with noise. You count six people, vaguely memorable from your old school days. They each re-introduce themselves to you one-by-one. These are people that you knew, but why can't you recognize any of them? They don't talk over each other nor do they break away into their own conversation. Everybody speaks in turn and always agrees with the previous speaker.

Eventually somebody tells a joke.

They all laugh.

Their smiles.

Their teeth.

Upstairs, there's more thumping, like somebody trying to break down a wall with their shoulder. The crying that accompanies it, while not familiar, feels almost nostalgic.

'It's that dog again,' you say. Everyone's looking at you. Nobody blinks. 'Or maybe your dad. You said he works from home, right? What does he do again?'

'He's not here,' Lacey says. 'Why would my parents be home on a girl's night?'

Everyone nods, agrees. Total unification.

It becomes all too much. 'Hey, Lace, can I use your bathroom? Last night was a little wild welcome home, and I'm still feeling it. If you know what I mean.'

'You know where it is,' Lacey says. 'Just don't take too long. I have a surprise for you.'

***

Honestly, you planned just to get the fuck out of Dodge. As the chatter dies when you exit the lounge, you know it is time to leave. Your quota for weird shit spilled over the threshold long ago, and now the voice in your head is making sense.

Leave.

Go away and never come back.

More noises from upstairs. It's louder this time, more intense than before. Something or someone really wants to leave.

You never were good at listening, even to your own conscience.

Sneaking to the second floor is a laborious process, hampered by the ever-present dread that someone will wonder what's taking so long. Maybe you should have shut the bathroom door when you passed it. You'll be caught in mere seconds if someone checks up on you.

You hit the landing on all fours, and gravitate to the one closed door among the rest. The rooms you pass are unfurnished. Completely empty.

It definitely sounds like sobbing.

There's no giant padlock, but the knob requires a key. You'd throw up a lock-picking video on your phone if you owned earbuds, but you're a headphones person and never bring those things to social events. No. Just you, a hairpin, and a dwindling allowance of time.

Your heart is beating so loudly in your ears that you wouldn't be able to hear footsteps in your direction until they touched you.

What feels like hours later, the thing finally clicks.

Inside is a dingily lit room with a boarded-up window, unfurnished except for a dirty mattress, a yet-to-be-emptied bucket of excrement, and a girl. Her nails are long, hair greasy, body just skin vacuum-sealed over her bones. She's backed into the corner and still retreating like caught prey.

It's instant recognition. You know only one person like that who can look that horribly unkempt.

'Lacey?' you ask. 'Like, are you the real one – no, no, no, don't cry. It's me, remember?'

You approach the girl with the same gentleness you'd use when coaxing a wild rabbit out of her den. It takes a bit, but she scrambles your way, then wraps her bony arms around you.

'What the hell happened to you?' you ask.

'I escaped," she eventually says. 'They had me, but I escaped.'

Your brows furrow. It was your mistake expecting something sensible from Lacey. 'You seem pretty confined to me.'

Lacey shakes her head. 'No, from there.' She points at the gap between the two-by-fours, at the measly backyard and the wilderness beyond the fencing. She's not making sense. 'But they need me alive. They need all of us alive.'

'Lace, who are they?'

As if by cue, a wash of light shines through the window and lights up the room. It's coming from the forest, a myriad of colours assaulting your eyes.

'You shouldn't be here,' Lacey says. A strange light leaks in from the back window, one that hurts your head to see. 'Leave me. Leave town. Before they come and steal you.'

Sounds reasonable enough. But it's not something you're going to do alone. You take Lacey's hand, and try to drag her with you. You've been gone too long. They must be suspicious by now. 'We escape together, then you can explain to me all this freaky shit that's going on.'

Seven pairs of eyes and seven plastic smiles greet your escape. All bundled-up together in the hall, like crayons in a box, you see how similar they all are. Person plagiarism.

'I don't think it's normal to snoop around someone's house,' Not-Lacey says.

'Like you know what that word means.' Before she can wedge a foot in, you slam the door in their faces.

Seven pairs of fists start knocking, beating so hard you can hardly think.

You yank your phone from your back pocket and fumble with the touch screen. 'We have to get out of here. Call the police or something. Or, or, how about this?' You tug at the two-by-fours blocking your escape. One can survive a second floor jump. Sure, broken bones are a guarantee, but adrenaline is wonderful, it can fix anything. If only the planks weren't nailed down so well. You grunt and strain, but the damn things refuse to move.

'This thing's not budging. Lacey, help me!'

She gets an A for effort, F in execution.

The woodland is alight with colour, a medley of shades and

hues that mash together like tie-dye. Anything in the light twists and curls. It tickles your arms, your face, but with such intensity that it reminds you of getting poked and prodded at a doctor's office. There's no warmth found in the rays, just a cold feeling of apprehension that grasps your spine.

You're grateful when it dies down, until you see what it leaves behind.

From the wilderness a nude figure, faceless, featureless, climbs over the fence from beyond. Its body morphs. Hair grows, eyes bubble up to the surface, a mouth tears open. It's a face you recognize. No piercings or moles or scars that should be there, but that face is one you'll never forget. After all, you see it every day in the reflection of your phone screen.

Lacey clings onto your arm tight. Wherever you go, she's coming with you.

So at least there's that.

The figure looks up. Smiles. Waves.

At least they got the teeth right on this one.

Witching Hour Radio

Sofia Reyes Valencia

Josué arrived to work at 9:00 p.m. He murmured his hello and clocked in behind the night watchman's desk, making idle chitchat about the weather, the watchman's wife and kids, and whether or not *el Tri* would actually make it to the final rounds of the world cup this year. Josué usually wasn't this approachable, but it was always good to be polite to the man in charge of keeping weirdos – and ugly fangirls – out of the studio. The man in question addressed him hesitantly.

'Say, Mr. Castillo, do you think that last call yesterday, from the old woman in Tehuacán, was real?' Josué smoothed down his tie and tried to remember what the older man was talking about. He hummed,

'You mean the lady who was worried her neighbor put a curse on her daughter's brand-new car?'

The watchman nodded,

'That's the one! I just bought a new car – well, used, but basically new. My wife's brother gave us an incredible deal on his old Cruiser. But I swear! The moment we parked it out in front of the driveway, there was a sudden chill in the air, and my wife says she saw the curtains in our front neighbor's windows move! Like someone had been watching! I bet you my wife's been bragging to the whole block about the new car – you know how women are—'

Josué laughed, 'No need to tell me.' He glanced at his watch:

ten minutes until he was on air. 'So, you're worried something similar is happening here?' The watchman shrugged, eventually nodded.

'That call just got me thinking; is it possible? What should I do? Is it the eye? Am I going to have to ask my in-law for my money back? We've already had some problems in the past, and my wife was telling me—'

'Woah, woah, woah! Slow down! Have you already hung a rosary on the rear-view mirror?'

The older man closed his mouth, eyes wide and surprised.

'I haven't! My God, that's the first thing I should have done! I know just the one too – there's this beautiful rosary my cousin brought us back from her trip to the Vatican. It's a beautiful piece, real gold plating.'

Josué nodded sagely,

'It sounds like just the thing. Make sure you get it blessed again before hanging it on the mirror. My late father had one in every car he owned, never had more than a small fender bender.'

'Of course! Why didn't I think of it sooner? Thank you, Mr. Castillo! Can't believe I've been so clueless. You know my wife's been making me drink a glass of green juice every morning – tastes absolutely horrible – but she says it's for your brain, overall health really, she says—' Josué laughed and clapped his hand on the man's shoulder.

He took a chance, 'Listen, Mr. Suarez,' the old man nodded again – *phew* – 'get your rosary blessed. Hang it up. Try taking some fish oil with your wife's juice.' The older man was nodding along to Josués advice, blissfully unquestioning. Before Suarez could respond, Josué walked past his desk – 'I'd love to talk more, but I'm sure Aléjandra's already waiting for me in the booth.' When he gave Suarez a genial smile, the man smiled back.

'Of course Mr. Castillo, of course! Thank you so much for all of your help. Have a good show!'

Josué was already halfway down the hall.

***

As expected, Alé was waiting for him in his chair. He closed the door behind him, sealing the booth, and she spun around, annoyed.

'Five minutes until we go live.'

He turned away from her to hang up his jacket.

'At least it's not one,' he said, turning around just in time to see the end of her eye-rolling.

'Right, well, Ricardo wants me to leave you without a producer today.' She scowled. 'Apparently his sister needs help installing her brand-new stereo system for a party they're throwing tomorrow!' she finished in an off-putting tone of fake cheer. He did his best to tune her out as she began another one of her 'Ricardo-Mendoza-Soto-is-a-jackass' rants, and double checked to make sure the audio levels and tapes were ready to go.

Josué liked Alejandra Tochtli well enough. She was a cute girl and a fine producer – even if she didn't always listen to his advice. A little loud, a little rude, sure, but who wasn't at her age? When Mr. Ruiz hired him, he too thought he would turn the station around, make some sort of positive change from the inside. In time Josué was sure she would learn the importance of the chain of command, of the way things were done around the radio station. Learning to respect the station's hierarchy had been one of the most difficult and most important lessons of Josué's career, and he hoped Ale wouldn't make the experience harder than it needed to be. After all, how would anyone else ever respect her if she always thought she was above paying her dues?

'—and do you remember that time he sent me out of our quarterly meeting to refresh his coffee? This is *just* like him, and if he thinks—'

'You should go.' She had begun to pace during her rant and now stopped to look at Josué as he took his seat in front of the mic. He shrugged. 'Your twenties are for doing people favors, you know? Petty, dumb shit other people are too lazy to deal with. I think you should do this for him.' She narrowed her eyes.

'You want me to ditch our show and help his teenage sister with her some fucking party prep?' He shrugged again,

‘Don’t be so emotional about it; this might finally put you in his good graces. Maybe he’ll even listen to some of your ideas on how to improve the show during our next meeting.’

Alé was outright glaring now.

‘You need a producer. It’s a call-in show.’

He gestured to the switchboard on his side of the desk,

‘That’s what this is for,’ he pressed on as she opened her mouth to reply. ‘Come on, it’s a Tuesday night, you know what this looks like by the third hour.’ He turned away from her and straightened his pile of ad copies. ‘Follow my advice for once and go do something nice for Ricardo. Grab your things quickly, too. My show’s about to start. He pulled on his headset and watched as the seconds ticked down to 9:15. He didn’t hear whatever she muttered as she shut the door to the booth.

***

‘Welcome back everyone, we’ve just entered the third hour of our paranormal communion – our haunted commiseration, if you will. This is Josué Velazquez Castillo, your faithful servant, as ever. It is fifteen minutes past midnight. Let’s see who’s on the line, shall we?’

Josué had been right – it had been a boring show. He talked an insistent grandmother down from double baptizing her grandchild, listened to an old man from San Martin as he recited what Josué was pretty sure had been the first half hour of *Close Encounters of the Third Kind* with the names and places changed, and he read a particularly corny ad for tuna fish. It would’ve been better for ratings to get something really out of the ordinary but, alas, it was all the usual ghosts, ghouls, and goblins. The night was quickly passing by, and he stubbed his eighth cigarette of the night out before continuing.

‘It’s 12:45 a.m., let’s take our last call of the night,’ he pressed the only flashing light left on the switchboard. ‘Hello caller, how about you tell us your name and location?’

There was a beat of silence. Then.

‘My name is Jimena. I’m calling from my home.’

Josué chuckled – first time callers were always adorable.

'Hello Jimena, how can I help you?' He tried to subtly modulate his voice, making it a little deeper and a little smoother. He liked it when younger women called in – it always made him sit up a little straighter, always made his voice feel a little more powerful, always made him feel more capable. He smiled as he heard her take a long breath in.

'I think I'm being haunted by some sort of demon.' She exhaled. He leaned back in towards his mic, interest piqued by the tone of her voice.

'That's a pretty big thing to be unsure about; demonic presences don't appear in half-measures. What makes you think so, Jimena?'

There was a static sound of shuffling on the other side of the line before she answered him. 'I've been having – strange thoughts. Thoughts I've never had before and—' she took another breath, and Josué's earphones amplified the sounds of air and static. 'Things keep happening around the house. Important papers: licenses, certificates, they aren't there when I look for them. I hear noises at night, like someone's walking up and down the halls, looking for something. Everytime I check, there's nothing there.' Josué felt himself nodding along with her voice, a little disappointed when she stopped.

'Well, those might all be examples of a classic haunting. It might all be a coincidence, of course. Have you been in good health? No sudden accidents or trauma? No head injuries?'

'I was in the hospital a few months ago,' she replied hesitantly, 'but that was at the start of the summer. These things only started happening at the beginning of the month.' That detail was interesting; usually, when people had these sorts of experiences, it was closely tied to a sudden bout of trauma or stress. He took the mic in his hand.

'Well, Jimena, that does seem strange. Have you been doing anything differently? Have you met anyone new, anyone particularly strange?'

'I've been looking for answers.' She did not elaborate.

'What kind of answers?' She was quiet. 'Jimena, dear? What kind of answers?'

'I—' she took another breath, 'I've been talking to a psychic. Last week I went to see a shaman. I've been trying to see someone who was taken from me.'

'What do you mean by taken, Jimena? Could you be more specific?'

'They died. They died before they should have.'

'I'm very sorry to hear that. Really, I am. Can you tell us who you're looking for?' He heard a shade of frustration in her voice when she replied,

'I don't think that matters. It's not what I called in to ask about.'

Josué had previously had difficult callers; people who were shy to elaborate but full of such an unshakeable conviction over their supernatural experience that they became resentful of his attempts to gather more information. If he could get a good story out of her tonight, though, all the extra work would be worth it. He centered himself and tried to make his voice more placating with his next question.

'Of course. I'm sorry for pressing you. Has there been anything else? Any other paranormal demonstrations?' He couldn't help but feel a little pleased when he heard the softness in her voice return.

'Yes.'

'Yes?'

More shuffling on her end of the line, maybe she was sitting up in bed, her satin sheets pooling around her body as she sat up – safe and soft at home. 'Yesterday, I was in the kitchen. I was making lunch, my mother-in-law and her sister were going to come over and eat with us. I was almost done with the *atole* we were going to have for after, when I heard someone knocking on the kitchen door.' Josué stubbed out his cigarette, letting himself be soothed by the cadence of her voice.

'Who was at the door, Jimena?' He was answered with another beat of silence, then,

'It was a little boy. A little boy and his brother. They were—' she swallowed quite audibly, 'they were dressed in rags, they had mosquito bites all over their arms and legs. They were so small.' She spoke in an almost breathy tone as she finished. For a moment, he felt as if it were just the two of them on a phone call.

'What did they say to you?'

'He apologized to me.' He heard her swallow again. 'He said he was so sorry, he knew I was probably busy, but his mother was sick, and they had no more food left in the house. He asked if I had anything in the cupboards I was thinking about throwing away. If I had anything I could spare for him and his brothers.' She was crying now. Josué's heart twinged in sympathy. Poor thing – it was always difficult to hear a woman cry. He did, however, relish the opportunity to offer her comfort.

'It's a sad state many people live in nowadays. I know that must have been difficult for you. It often is, for women who have such good hearts. But, Jimena, why do you think this has something to do with your haunting?' His ears thrummed as he felt the vibrations of her crying.

'Because—' she started, 'because I told them to stay put. I told them I was going to go back inside to pack up some things for them to take. I packed away everything I had on the stove, a handful of cans from the cupboards and a loaf of bread. I took all of it outside, I was in the middle of asking him if he needed help taking it all back home when I realized they were gone.' She let out a shuddering sob. 'I walked up and down the path that leads to our kitchen door. I asked our neighbors if they had seen anything, no one had. I called out for them; I left the food out on the stoop to see if anyone would come back for it. I went back outside, late at night, and the food was still untouched. Even the strays that nose around our garbage every week had left it alone.' Josué leaned forward again, forearms resting on the edge of the desk as both hands now gripped his mic. In the back of his mind, he registered a faint knocking at the door of the booth.

'Jimena, I don't think—' she cut him off before he could finish.

'And now? Now I hear children laughing in the middle of the night. I hear them, for hours on end, as if they were playing right outside my window. No one believes me when I try to tell them about it, not even my husband.' She had stopped crying very suddenly. She sounded angry. 'I ask him and I ask him. I beg him to stay up with me to hear them when they come and it's always a different excuse. I know he's been talking to his family, to his mother. He denies it when I ask him, but I know.'

'Jimena, dear, try to breathe for me, okay? You're safe, you're at home! I need you to—'

'No! No, no, no, no!' Her voice was shrill. 'Everyday. Every single goddamn day, I am so, so *angry*. I am so *sick* of living like this. Like I'm crazy, like I'm – I'm—'

'Jimena—' he tried to make his voice sound stern. He couldn't understand why his body had broken out into a cold sweat. The knocking became louder.

'Shut up!' she snapped. She was breathing like some sort of angry, caged beast. 'There's something inside me, now. Something that I invited in, and now it's made me see how wrong everyone else is. How blind. How fake. How stupid,' she laughed. 'I see it. I see them, and I see you too. Why lie to your poor watchman? Why not tell him your father was a lifelong atheist? Why not tell Alejandra you think she's too stupid to do her job, hm?' Her voice dripped with something evil then. 'Why not just admit to yourself that you like the feeling of control? You like the feeling of all these people listening, hanging onto your every word? You live for calls like this – some poor, stupid, pretty thing to come running to you for help! Why not tell the truth? Why not put it all on the table?' His mouth opened and closed. He felt the vibrations of someone knocking against the door of the booth to the roots of his teeth.

'Jimena, please—' she laughed at him again. The knocking grew stronger, angrier.

'I'm not here anymore, Josué,' she was cackling, 'I'm not here! I'm not here! I'm not here!' Again and again, wilder and wilder.

The lights in the booth went out. His blood ran cold. The door banged open.

If Macbeth Was A Woman

Milly Sweeney

My weary Kinsmen, hark, for I hath words.
This sword imprints on ambiguous necks
That bear minds flooded, frenzied and forlorn,
By storm clouds brewing in our Scotland's skies.
If thy ambitious, enterprising soul
Seeks to repair, as nurses must to wounds,
Or council as a mother would to a babe,
She would be mocked a fortnight into next.
This chest-born laughter deep and gruff in tune,
A melody that's known to women's ear.
And so when opportunity appears,
Like rainfall in the lowly summer drought,
Tis' not approach-ed calmly and with care
But rather met with claws, and sabotage.
If thou does beat her sisters to the crown,
Her lavish life cannot be yet enjoyed.
For coupled with the guilt of her assent,
Her country's people pick apart her rule.
With jealous talons rip into her being
A jezebel, an angel and a bitch.
If her demeanour's perceived as aloof,
A fiery fate awaits the country's witch.

An Intermission

As, first, good company, good wine, good welcome,
Can make good people.

Henry VIII I • 4

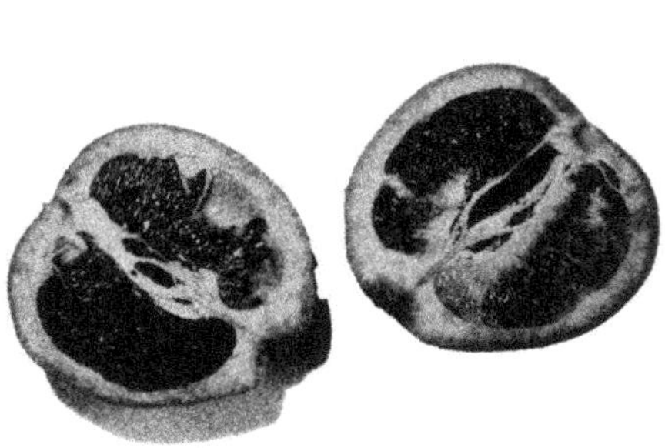

At this time, please feel free to take a brief respite. Stretch your legs, grab a snack, or a drink. Perhaps try our recommended cocktail, The Paloma. Instructions and ingredients are listed below.

The Paloma

The classic margarita's more exciting relative, the Paloma, is a wonderful combination of sour, salty, and sweet. The blending of sharp citrus with heady tequila, nulled ever so slightly by the saccharine syrup, makes for a light and fresh drink that satisfies even in the colder months – which, if you're in Scotland, like us, makes up most of the year.

But the best thing about a Paloma is that no cocktail equipment is required, and you can experiment with what ingredients are available to you, for example, soda can be exchanged for sparkling water, honey for simple or agave syrup, and the tequila can be removed entirely for an alcohol-free alternative.

Simply salt your highball or coupe glass (if you're feeling fancy) by rubbing the rim of the glass with lime or grapefruit and dip. To a beaker or jug, add all the ingredients along with plenty of ice and stir. Sweeten to taste and pour into your desired glass to serve. Add ice if you're using a highball, refrain with your coupe or it will literally overfloweth.

Ingredients – serves one
50ml tequila
10ml honey
10ml lime juice (roughly half a squeezed lime)
60ml grapefruit juice
soda or sparkling water
salt, to garnish

Alcohol-Free Paloma
60ml grapefruit juice
10ml lime juice
Soda or sparkling water
10ml honey
Salt, to garnish
Optional, 50ml alcohol-free tequila. Provides all the flavour with none of the anxiety.

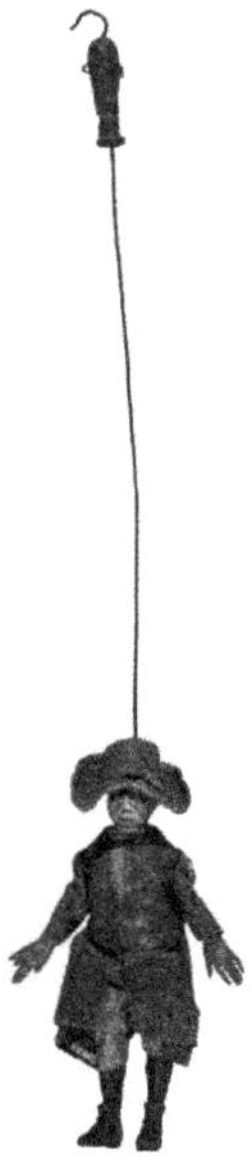

Act IV

O, let me not be mad, not mad, sweet heaven;
Keep me in temper; I would not be mad!

King Lear I • 5

Contemporary Companion

Barlow Crassmont

You just can't let It go. You're a weakling, a feeble being, a spineless omnivore incapable of fortitude.

You can put It down occasionally, you can ignore Its shiny, glossy features for a few minutes. You can even turn It off during the night, ensuring the extension of Its life in the long run. But the instant your ears pick up the chirping of the birds with the rising sun, your eyelids' foggy optics search for only one thing. Lying on the bed stand, so forlorn and inoperative, It stares back at you, like the endless abyss, and, if you listen carefully enough, you can even hear Its alluring call: whispering, singing, reciting the most seductive poetry, daring your temptation to get the best of you.

You weren't always such an invertebrate. When you were young, your father held your sweaty hand, comforting you from the fresh scrape on your bloody knee, assuring you it was gonna be alright.

It's nothing. Just a scratch, champ. A battle scar. You'll be a better man for it someday.

But it burns, you said, your eyes welling up.

That's just the thing, champ. You're free to take chances and try new things while playing. Nothing better in this world. Cherish that while you can. It goes away with the onset of years.

Cherish that ability. Who wouldn't?

You're free to do what you want, to see who you want, to go

where you want, and to be whomever you want, and your device only gets in the way. An unnecessary distraction from a social life whose substance should be people and friendships and relationships and memories of human interaction, not some hand computer. You're not taking It with you to the *West End Tavern.* No, definitely not.

Instead, you will listen to what your friends have to say. When was the last time you actually *listened* to Eddie tell you about his son's little league results? Or to Lance, as he explains his fascinating ideas about the new software he's working on? Or to Walter, as he shares his sorrow from his recent divorce? They're beings of flesh and blood, of heart and mind, and you need to show them the proper attention and kindness when listening, just as they do to you. *That's* what you'll be doing. The phone will stay at home, on your bed stand.

Well, maybe not all the way there. Maybe It can go in your pocket, untouched. You'll just shut It off, and take It with you, but won't be turning It on or looking at It.

Not. At. Anytime. That's it.

At long last, become the free man your father hoped you would.

***

The bar is raucous, stuffy, and loud. Walter and Eddie are already here, both grinning as they shake your hand. Despite the cordial atmosphere and the communal aura of the tavern, all you see is the select few in the background who are detached from human interaction. One man giggles as he reads a funny message. A woman smiles while playing a video, and shows it to her friend, who laughs. These people came out to socialize, to drink away their problems, to share with their fellow man the warmth of conversation and personal understanding. Instead, they're in cyberspace, isolated, severed from the physical and spiritual closeness one can get from human eye contact. You pity them, the poor fools.

Your hand goes into your pocket, and fondles your device. But it's ok, you're not tempted, you're just showing It who's boss. The fingertips stroke Its smooth glass, and eventually, through no fault of your own, your forefinger unwittingly turns on the button, accidentally. The powered screen's illumination is visible through your pocket, and although you try to play it off as an accident, Walter and Eddie see right through you.

A man with a hook in lieu of a hand orders a mojito behind your table. Protruding out of his wrist, the curved metal craftily pulls out and puts away the money from his back pocket wallet. You stare at the prosthetic with some apprehension, trying to imagine a different device impaled in the hook's place. As a convenience, it would go a long way.

Here comes Lance, dressed as a hipster-professor, his pullover aging him ten years. You use his arrival to distract yourself from It, and put your hand on the table, far away from the temptation zone. Walter asks Lance about his latest project.

It's a new Multi-Experience Version 3.8, a fully immersive technology.

Really?

Blah blah blah…

Oh yeah?

Blah blah…

That's interesting. How's blah blah blah?

A profound conversation. You're not certain which you'll lose first: your aching brain, overpowered by the vociferous noise of senseless chatter and incomprehensible lyrics whose only purpose, apparently, is to echo infinitely between each eardrum; or your restless hands, jittering, shaking, trembling, in desperate need of technological fulfillment. You keep your head up, pretending to listen to the trio's miseries, frustrations, confessions and the like, hoping your staged attentive demeanor will force them to look away from the pocket of your pants, where your hand just dove in, with gluttonous zeal.

Your fingers envelop the cuboid shape, sliding up and down the long edge of the glass, gently rubbing, stroking, fondling. You feel the warmth of the lit screen, the glow injecting your fingertips with sensual delight. Soon your heartbeat intensifies, and you're feeling a sensuous fire in your loins, the rising libido levels unusually rapid, abrupt, nearly overpowering. Your friends laugh at a joke Walter just cracked, and you join in, ardently pretending to be in on it, when, at this very moment, at the edge of a euphoric peak, you've no idea what day it is. The giggling and the shared laughter only aids in your present elation. You're well aware that if you don't excuse yourself to attend to the matter privately, you may never live it down.

I'm gonna hit the head, you say to the trio, then sprint to the restroom.

Luckily, it's a small, one-person-at-a-time toilet and sink combo. You pull out your mighty device, Its aura overwhelming you with a sensation of chills, the hairs on your arms standing, like a block of armed forces saluting an otherworldly monolith. As you release a much delayed – but subdued – *Aaaaaah*, the acoustical reverberation dissipates within the walls. At least, you hope.

On the device, several messages are unanswered. You frantically scroll, and begin typing responses even before you've finished reading them. There are new posts, comments and statuses on Face, Insta, Snap and Twit. These must be tended to immediately, without delay. It won't take long. They won't mind. They're busy conversing. Poor bastards.

By the time you reappear, only Eddie is left, finishing his fourth or fifth pint. His eyes are unfocused, head slightly wobbling.

Where you been this long? His words are slurred.

***

A few days is all it takes for your shame to set in. It's a delayed remorse, the kind one feels after a pointless argument with an absolute stranger. Instead of apologising and engaging in diplomacy at the outset, you pour additional fuel on the fire, until the flame swallows your dignity, pride and decency. Highlights only the thoughtlessness, which is to be your defining feature.

You call Walter, and leave him a half-assed message, telling him how sorry you are that your stomach started to act up at the worst possible time. He responds quicker than you could have anticipated.

But you were gone for more than an hour, he says.

Have you ever had chronic diarrhea? No response. *Didn't think so.*

Lance answers after the third ring. He acknowledges each part of your atonement with his signatory, *Mm-hm*. You feel he may have already given up when it comes to you. His indifference is glaring, his disregard palpable.

To your parting, *I'll see you around*, he says nothing at all, and when you hang up, you wonder why he never said *bye*.

Had he already terminated the call? Either way, you're down to two friends, which is plenty. It's more than one, at least. And even *one*, if it came down to it, would be sufficient.

News reports the story of a man who impaled himself with his device. His arm bleeds out before reaching the hospital, discouraging those who would've followed in his footsteps, had he succeeded. The story goes viral, nearly breaking the web.

You shake your head and *tsk* at the spineless masses. *Fucking amateurs. The world's getting weaker by the day.*

Free of the bro/buddy burden, you try online dating and spend countless hours looking at profiles, swiping this way and that, before finally arriving at a woman of interest: Claudia, from Vermont. A brunette, late twenties, enjoys 'Sex and the City,' Margaret Atwood, and parasailing during summer. Her texts are clever and engaging, her sense of humour dark, but not appalling. She makes you giggle often, and smile excessively.

At first you're reserved, demure, hesitant to open up. But as she peels each layer of her inviting personality, you reciprocate. You talk about the redundancy of your job, your disgruntlement with modern technology, and the obstacles of phone addiction for present humans. She agrees, confiding in you her own regretful dependence on the tiny black mirror, and the difficulty of ignoring its seductive call. She hopes to one day put it down for good, to leave its destructive nature behind, never to resume it again. You share her sentiments, and she hearts your *You and me both* message in the thread. She is the woman you've been waiting for, the saviour who will, at long last, help you slay the indomitable fixation to which you've been enslaved. You will simply toss It, unwavering, as an enlightened junkie does a pipe that's possessed his small, brittle body for way too long.

Claudia agrees to meet for coffee next Saturday. You'll leave It at home this time, far away from any human interaction. No more powered-off devices sitting harmlessly in the pocket. You've failed that test too many times.

In person, Claudia strikes you as genuine, polite and kind. Her friendly eyes appear interested, and her handshake is warm and gentle, her palm pleasantly free of sweat. You're amazed at how quickly the cheerful greeting evolves into comfortable, shared laughter over the complexity of the parking lot, and how the echo of the chuckles pleasantly fades into a conscientious conversation about the difficulty of modern dating.

Too many dull men, freaks, and perverts, she says.

You nod, *that's what I've heard.*

Two tables behind Claudia, in the background, a woman answers her ringing phone. Your eyes witness this without looking over. The conversation grows loud, drowning out anything Claudia says to your impressionable ears. You grow distracted, glancing back and forth between the two contrasting women, unsure of which one is worthier of your attention. Your fingers twiddle and fret, but they've nothing to hold onto or grab to douse the uncontrolled twitching. If only it was here with you now, resting at the end of your left arm, the metal rod taking the place of your useless fist.

If only.

Your mind wanders, any noise reaching it coming off as dreadful drivel, slowed down tenfold. Claudia glances down at your active hands, a look of concern emitting from her brown eyes. If you can only muster enough resistance to stay, to combat this dominant frailty before it takes over completely, you'll be a more complete, soulful human in the long run, someone that Claudia could respect, spend time with, perhaps even cherish some day. But alas, the distortion of present coherence, the mutation of absorbed speech and language around you, the uncontrollable craving devouring and turning over your spineless gut, is too much to bear.

You stand up, and say not another word – *What would be the point anyway?* – then simply walk away. Turning the corner and escaping her sight behind the adjacent building overwhelms you with delayed relief.

***

By the time you sprint home and your hand reaches for It on the white bed stand, you're barely able to keep yourself from full-on hyperventilation. The sweaty face, the rapid heart rate, the shivering hands: all necessary after effects of the crucial gratification. You fall backwards on your vacant bed, the device glowing and vibrant in your emaciated hands. Night envelops you on all sides, seeping through your vision, until the screen is the only thing perceptible in the absolute darkness. It fills you with joy, comfort and delight that people, for all their passion and tenderness, no longer can.

***

Minutes pass, then hours. Who cares? Time is irrelevant, for the present nirvana is preferable to any other sensation known.

You chug the bottle of brandy like it's a soft drink, and you see your reflection off the cleaver laying on the bedside table. Several more swigs should get you numb enough to minimize the forthcoming pain. The metal rod that will connect It to the severed stump is good and ready, shinier than a silver coin. Prevention of excessive blood loss is of utmost priority, so it's a good thing you've gauze and morphine and melting wax to go around. The bloody stubble will hurt, but no more than a tooth extraction, sans novocaine. At least you'll never again be deprived of your one and only. No more forgot it here, misplaced it there, and left it who knows where. It will become a part of you, more useful than that useless appendage: the left hand.

But here comes a notification reminder.

And another still.

Followed by several more.

Should check each of them first – for some things cannot wait.

Blood Roses

Alice Eaves

(after 'Karen' by Jessica Harrison)

You asked me to be everything
and nothing all at once

pure diamond for your mother
and wolfish in the sheets

a lady built for pleasure
with lips sewn shut

be a good girl
learn to control that *mouth*

for it was words that scared you
        but when will enough be enough?

when I have what no one else can
you spat onto my spine

so I gave it to you
like a new-born pulled from my cunt

you don't want it now
and it's a bit too late for that

Fabian Dysart

Douglas Thompson

You will recall my face quite easily, I believe, a well-known actor and household name I was, scarcely more than a decade ago.

But the moment I saw the now infamous episode of the soap opera *Mean City*, I instructed my agent to initiate legal action. Most of you probably already know the setting of *Mean City*: a mythical street in Glasgow in a 'transitional' area where working class families have been mostly displaced by well-to-do middle-class retirees. Who in turn are being infiltrated by nouveau riche yuppies, some of whom might conceivably be the original working-class inhabitants made good after university degrees. That, or a lucky run on the National Lottery. In Scotland, the posher you are, the more English you sound – strange, but true. A long-standing national identity crisis. The social tensions between the diverse households living on *Mean City*'s Humberland Street are the stuff of high comedy and too-close-to-home cringe. *Mean City* is not so much a sex comedy as a class comedy, not so much a sitcom as a Scotcom. Skitcom, shitcom.

The slur against me was unprovoked. An older pompous character they introduced to save their falling ratings, he had a plummy accent clearly an impersonation of my own. The one that I had gained while pacing the boards of RADA and the Old Vic.

Fabian Dysart, they called him. A ridiculous-sounding name, probably some complex anagram of my own. He had moved into flat 4B in the architect-designed Redux Apartments the week before, becoming the subject of curtain-twitching speculation as he carried in various items of fashionable furniture to his new pad. Cornered by his new neighbour, long-standing *Mean City* favourite Annabel Lamont, he was lured into a coffee shop (the wittily named Bump n' Grind) to divulge his life story. Here things quickly got libellous. Describing himself as a retired and vaguely disgraced actor, Fabian rhymed off the names of various films he'd had significant parts in, which were only *slightly* different from my own CV – *Star Watch, The Phantom Grimace, Ohio Smith and the Temple of Gloom, The Anger Games: Poppinjay, Legs Wide Closed, and Total Default.*

To my great surprise the reaction of the producers to my legal injunction wasn't outrage, ridicule or arch defensiveness, but an invitation relayed through my agent for me to come and visit the production team on set.

I pondered for a day or two. I positively prevaricated. I closed the curtains and vigorously procrastinated. I took council on my pillow, for a few nights, or at least one. The newspapers would soon learn of the fuss I was kicking up. This was my *I'm A Celebrity Get Me Out Of Obscurity* moment. Would this be the signal for my lauded return to the limelight, or to public ridicule and humiliation? Either way, I thought, I always was a sucker for attention.

Their set-up down there was impressive, I have to admit. It had somehow never occurred to me that the buildings on the famous street were mostly plywood facades, unrelated to the interior rooms which were staged in a warehouse nearby. They showed me how the entire street could be accelerated towards sunset and nightfall at the flick of a switch, with a glowing moon rising up on a gantry with cotton wool clouds sailing across it at the whim of the director, Des Chisolm. Des shook my hand vigorously, a sly smirk on his face and a twinkle in his eye, neither of which I could quite trust or decipher.

As I strolled down their artificial street bathed in the glare of a floodlight sun, Des introduced me to their producer, an overweight transport magnate with a habit of dabbling clumsily in local politics. This impudent impresario slapped my back then made a suggestion which truly floored me: 'Why don't you come and join the cast? This is our scriptwriter Larry right here, we could get him to write you in.' Larry duly emerged from behind the film crew, head wagging over his clip-board like a nodding dog in bottle-bottom specs.

'How on earth would that work?' I asked. 'Two versions of me confronting each other in the bathroom mirror or something?'

Des's laugh was like an unblocked drain, and his white teeth flashed. 'Our Larry will think of something. Wait and see.'

I should have kept a recording of that conversation and sued them. Again. For stealing my idea this time, not just my voice and acting style. Did I nod back in agreement without meaning to? Did I let the quality of the wines they plied me with over our subsequent lunch numb my senses and lull me into witless complacency and compliance?

In the next episodes they started the process of gradually changing the character of Fabian Dysart. He began unnerving long-term resident and *Mean City* favourite Bruce Bentley through various conversations as they passed in the street. Turns out clean-cut classically handsome Bruce had been an actor once too, an old fellow thespian. The way it was scripted, Bruce and Fabian began by talking cautiously like old friends accidentally reunited, vaguely wary of each other. As their differing memories were drawn out over numerous conversations, things gradually turned darker, as Fabian begins to hint at, and then actually does, blackmail Bruce – 'Do you remember all the drugs we used to take back in the day, Bruce? All the girls, the boys? What about your current wife, Samantha, isn't it? What if she were to be told about that orgy we had back in 1998 at Sandy Groznick's place? Remember? He was a high-flying producer back then, before all those ugly allegations of underage sex and child molestation crept in…'

Each week as Fabian got more threatening, viewers began to suspect that his sole motive in buying a flat in the street was to stalk and torment Bruce. The very appearance of Tavish Louthwaite, the actor playing Fabian, seemed to slowly change. He became more visibly evil, half demon, and he seemed to be descending into paranoid schizophrenia. All of this culminates in a pivotal scene in his ensuite bathroom where the reflection in the mirror ceased to be Tavish and finally became yours truly. My debut in

Mean City, my long overdue return to the small screen.

Thereafter, Tavish was replaced by myself, and Fabian Dysart became my first substantial acting role in seven years. I felt exhilarated, rehabilitated, vindicated. But even though I was back in business, there was a sour taste in my mouth. Were the script writers ridiculing me? Was I ridiculing myself? All those references to past scandals were a tad near the bone. Like some spreading stain of black ink, once darkness creeps in, it is seldom easy to contain, let alone mop up.

Fabian's blackmail of Bruce Bentley continued, and the ratings went up. Soon I was a household name once more. Des Chisholm offered me my own luxury trailer, on set so I could immerse myself more in the role. A co-credit in writing and directing were dangled like proverbial carrots. Larry shadowed me night and day to note down points from the endless discussions between Des and I on character development. Sometimes criminal psychologists and sociologists were brought in to comment on character development. They asked me what Fabian would do next. As if I might have already developed a unique understanding of his character. As if I could become him. As if I *was* him.

Living on set also suited me for other reasons. I wanted my return to the camera glare to be on my own terms. I eschewed interviews after a few cheeky hacks tried to bend the questions around to whether I had ever met the family of Bernardo Gonzalez or paid them damages for the tragic incident at my Lanzarote poolside. 'The incident for which I was wholly cleared and acquitted?' I responded testily from behind my Gucci dark glasses.

Meanwhile Fabian Dysart was not content with blackmail. Not content with causing Bruce Bentley to descend into alcohol and drug abuse. Not content with making Bruce's marriage fracture under the stress of his threats, and so Fabian became more dangerous still. It seemed that the audiences loved this, and demanded more of it. As if I inhabited a virtual coliseum and was circled by a baying crowd, a gladiator in the ascendant, presided over by emperor Des. A smart parasite should never destroy its host, only endlessly weaken it.

But as we see in nature, it rarely works out like that. Fabian eventually bit too hard, and Bruce became desperate. Talked of going to the police. The script began to make it clear that Fabian was ultimately murderous in intent. As if blackmail had only been the half of it. As if he was driven by some profound jealousy of Bruce's relative wealth and hitherto idyllic home life.

I played the part brilliantly, if I do say so myself, even hinting at some kind of sublimated long-term homoerotic crush. As if Fabian wanted to become Bruce, replace him, steal all that he owned. In a climactic scene, scheduled to air on Christmas Eve so as to thrash all other soap competitors in the ratings war, Bruce turned on me. It was during a meeting on a remote hilltop in Argyll, in which he was to hand over a suitcase of used cash. Hands around my neck in tears of desperation, he has me in a throttle. Demands that I stop hounding him and leave his wife and kids alone. Leave the street, use the cash to buy a flat in some other city, return to London, or wherever I'd been hiding for the previous decades honing my grudges. As the camera zooms in, a knife falls from Bruce's pocket, one he brought to threaten me with. Before the viewers even have time to think on the intentions of their wholesome hero, my outreached hand finds the blade's handle and thrusts it into Bruce's side. The nation flinches, dropping their remote controls, clutching their half-boiled pots of potatoes, putting down their half-dried dishes, gather around their screens in disbelief.

Of course, uncertainty over whether Bruce would survive his wound were drawn out over as many subsequent episodes as possible. Touch and go in intensive care, family members gathered around the bedside, hoping he'd regain consciousness, preparing their goodbyes.

Fabian is back on the street, feigning horror to all his fellow residents over Bruce. They've all been fooled into thinking that he's become one of Bruce's best pals over the last few months, the scoundrel. There's a nail-biting scene where Fabian visits Bruce in the hospital. When no other relatives are there, and the nurse leaves the room, I pick up a pillow and start to smother him before a doctor walks in, and I just manage to pull off a swift diversion worthy of a stage magician. I leave the sleeping Bruce, still alive, and my guilt unsuspected. Crimes only known to the viewers as if they are the mind of an omnipresent God, all seeing and all judging. As they so love to be.

Bruce rallies and recovers. I have to hand it to Larry, he wrote the episodes well…a writer getting into his stride. Bruce begins dropping hints to his nearest and dearest and the police. And by the very measure by which he recovers, it seems that Fabian's mental health begins to deteriorate. Beset with guilt and paranoia, Fabian imagines everyone on the street starting to suspect him. There are whispers in his head, and he imagines movement in the corners of his vision, twitching hands, people making secret signs to each other that he is rumbled, caught out, that they are recording him on their mobiles, phoning the police.

These peripheral manifestations gradually become black spiders, rats, and other unspeakable creatures, emissaries of darkness gnaw at the edges of Fabian's brain, feasting on the folds of his cerebellum, his occipital lobe. Now it's Fabian's turn to resort to drinking heavily, struggling to sweat out these demons that hound him night and day.

The police interview various residents of the street. They're like dumb, slow and meandering bloodhounds. Episode after episode they blunder, but they continuously draw irrevocably closer to the trail of sweat that leads back to Fabian, a scent of corruption that can never be lost or shaken off.

I had hoped that an award or two might be in the offing for my performance. Hell, if it had been a Hollywood film, then perhaps an Academy Award, an Oscar, an Emmy. Right before Bruce returns home in his recovery wheelchair, Fabian finally loses it. He slopes off into the night and wanders the neighbouring districts in a state of bewilderment for a week and a half, progressively becoming a wino, a beggar, a down-and-out. It was powerful stuff. Socially responsible drama. Helplines were offered at the end of the episodes for sensitive viewers who had been affected by issues similar to those raised in the programme, the poor little dears. In order to immerse myself totally in the part, I went completely method. I gave up showers and shaving, all personal hygiene. Forsook my comfortable trailer on set for sleeping on benches in nearby parks. Word got out and sightings of me began to be reported all over the city, few of which could actually have been me. Numerous tramps were asked for their autographs, some even had money offered for them. By that measure at the very least, I did some good in the world.

Tonight, I shuffled and swayed down this street, sniffing like a crepuscular fox at the entrance to every alleyway, looking for dog-ends to pick up and smoke, rifling through bins to find half-eaten burgers and fish suppers to smear my face with. I found half a bottle of Buckfast and slugged it back, howling like a wolf at the moon.

I could have sworn that the corner of that building I just leant against swayed under my weight. I hope the cameras didn't pick that up. I really must have a word with the set designers, tell them to get the carpenters back in to patch up and strengthen the scaffold that supports this flimsy stage set of false facades.

In fact, I go back now to examine the building I stubbed my toe on and am confused to find that it gives off no tell-tale hollow ring, that it is in fact made of very solid, very old and heavy stone, elaborately carved.

'Des! Larry! Switch that floodlight moon on, will you? Come here and take a look at this!'

What's the world coming to when even a seasoned actor like me can no longer be certain of what is fantasy and what is real and where one bleeds and fades into the other?

I keep on walking, staring straight ahead to keep the spiders and rats at bay in peripheral vision, in the gutters, running up and down rainwater pipes. They don't scare me if I stay in control, show them who's boss.

There's an art to it, this acting thing. A child's make-believe that even adults are fooled by. To tell a great lie, you must first believe it yourself. But like making a false face into the wind, as our mothers used to warn us: might it not stick one day if we are not careful?

'Can you spare some change, mate? Just a few coppers so I can buy coffee or lunch. What's that, you don't carry any cash any more these days? I look familiar to you? You will recall my face quite easily I believe, well-known actor and household name as I was scarcely more than a decade ago. But strange to report, come to think of it now: that name, I can no longer remember myself.'

The Audient Void

R. M. McRitchie

Lysander understands he is not free.

He escapes through the whooshing automatic doors, wearing his cap and threadbare duster jacket once more, now a touch looser at the sleeves. The stench of bleach and recycled air fade behind him, but the chemicals have done their work. They've scorched inside his nostrils.

To the porters, he is not the same man they wrestled into mint nylon scrubs a mere three months ago. Calm, sensible, well behaved – he is as I instructed him to be. It was the quickest way to stop the electric shocks and avoid golden afternoons wasted in that drab common room painting fruit bowl tableaus.

They hoped art therapy might resonate with him. No one listened when he told them he despised visual art. 'Paintings are dull, static, impassive productions,' he'd said. 'Viewers consume them like junk food – mindless and in bulk – at their hushed galleries. Once the paints dry, no smell exudes from them, and you risk a ban if you dare touch a masterpiece behind its velvet rope.' Never had he seen them move an audience to overwhelming emotion or, more importantly, to action. In his opinion, they were pointless.

So, upon my advice, he devised his own treatment programme in his preferred art form: theatre. Every day Lysander played the part of a model inmate, telling the psychoanalyst what they wanted to hear, smoothing wrinkles from his nylon, swallowing his bitter pills without argument.

His convincing performance bewildered his attendants. They frowned as they reviewed his notes: *admitted kicking and screaming*. Now, they had to concede, there was no reason to hold Lysander at all. This was a different man from the one who'd entered Wilde-Welkin Reformation Centre.

Zoe thinks the same, relieved at the change. She waits by the chain-link fence and gives a small wave when she spots him coming out of the hospital. As he plods toward her, she notes his deep-set eyes – akin to the dark sockets of a skull – and that his cheeks are gaunter. She wishes he'd pick up the pace.

Grey concrete blocks towering over the street are stifling, giving the air that stale and soupy consistency she associates with mid-city afternoons. Prolonged exposure leaves her breathless, and the feeble flicker of the yellow street lamps is bringing on a headache.

'You alright, Antonin?' She tries to appear unbothered, dropping her hands into the front pocket of denim dungarees she's too old to pull-off nowadays.

'I told you in the letter. It's Lysander.'

'Right, right. Just – I'm not sure a new name will stop them finding you if they want to, I mean, if you try anything.' A pause. 'You're not going to, are you? Try again?'

'Of course not, I'm done with all that.' Lysander aims a precise, glistening globule of spit at the pavement, missing his smart shoes by an inch. They haven't lost their shine from the night of the preview, not after the months suspended in a patient locker.

He doesn't flinch as Zoe touches his forearm and gives him a weak smile. 'Good. I'd prefer not to see them haul you away again, you know. Expect they'll keep a closer eye on you, after rocking the boat.'

Lysander fights the scowl that threatens to upset his disguise.

They already are, he imagines telling her. *They've sent you.*

Same pixie nose, a freckle dot by her left ear – this figure *looks* like Zoe, and sounds like her too. *But it can't be her*, Lysander convinces himself. Zoe trusted him. She supported every crazy trend or experiment he brought to her secret little theatre above the abandoned community hall. His creative genius drew in the crowds and she, the strongest artistic freedom fighter around, took a chance on everything radical. She lived for any opportunity to stick up a middle finger to the Man. They were the perfect pairing.

But this isn't Zoe, he thinks, and shudders. He wonders how they created this doppelgänger. None of the usual grapevine channels were chattering about a new form of government spy. It could be a person with cosmetic enhancements, a sophisticated android, something in between. He quells the musings and hopes never to find out. Any answer is too bleak when he considers what they've done with the real Zoe.

Instead, he decides to bait the imposter, force her to commit to her part, and denounce her creators. '*You* liked it though, didn't you? Although you're not supposed to.' He spins up a grin, a hint of the man he used to be.

The question transports her. Lysander cannot see it, but I do – how she fears even to blink. She knows she will face that infamous preview performance behind her eyelids for the millionth time since his imprisonment. It plagues her dreams, haunts her stray thoughts. And she is not the only one. They all endure it. Everyone who attended that show. Zoe met a few for coffee and saw her own dark bags and red-veined stares mirrored back at her. They'd been trying to forget; she'd triggered them with her curiosity, but she had to know she wasn't alone, that *she* shouldn't be detained at Wilde-Welkin too.

'It was something,' she replies, pitching a light-hearted tone. 'Once in a lifetime.' She hopes.

Her skin stipples. Someone is breathing on her neck so she turns, glances up and down the street. She flinches, expecting to glimpse the midnight cloaks fluttering in the breeze as in her dream, where their wearers pierce her inner world with chartreuse stares. But the city is empty of life, and it's still day, not the infinite starry eventide of her nightmares. The sun, faint greenish in the sickly sky, cannot warm her chilled bones. She wraps her arms around herself in an embrace.

'Well?' Lysander interrupts her agitation. 'Should we get going?'

Zoe starts, blinks as if she'd forgotten he was there. 'Oh, yeah. My car's parked this way.'

She leads him from the Reformation Centre, toward the multi storey carpark, jangling her keys while spinning them on her finger. Their clinking fills the quiet with a lonely music, and Lysander finds himself humming an accompaniment. *That* song, *my* song – the one he heard on his trip over-shores last year, the earworm that lives in his brain. In the hospital, it had been a comfort and companion for his new persona.

He clamps his lips closed to seal it away. A sidelong glance at Zoe's distant expression assures him she did not notice. He exhales. She, unlike the doctors, could recognise the melody from the preview night. He mustn't hum or whistle or tap it on a surface, mustn't risk blowing his cover and dash any hope of a second run. His teeth are nervously chattering by the time they reach Zoe's rust-brown sedan.

Soon. He promises me and the version of himself that hides in his mind's shadows. *The show must go on.*

***

When Zoe drops him off at his flat, he doesn't stay long. They've turned over his belongings as he expected – bookshelves barren, typewriter impounded, records smashed to splinters in their slipcases.

He sits on the lumpy, discoloured mattress for a moment, breathing in the mingled smells of ink and black mould – familiar to any pauper artist's home – and considers his next move. *Dancers, musicians, mimes*, that's what he needs. *The best in the business.* His red rotary phone is still intact at least, so he fetches his address book from its hiding place under a loose kitchenette tile. Picks up the receiver, and stalls. The telltale click of a bugged line meets his ear.

He smirks. It's as I'd warned him. They believe this clean-up job will deter him. So accustomed are they to citizens rolling over for their scare tactics. Weak, stupid dependents that need, that *want*, the government to direct their lives for them.

Well, not me, thinks Lysander.

The cafe is three blocks and a short metro ride south. Keeping his head ducked, he affects a trudge that mimics the soul-crushed labourers shuffling around him. Pretending is enough for their misery to rub off on him, to coat his skin with the slime of factory grease or the gritty soil of chemically saturated fields. The artificial gravity of it drags his bones into the ground, makes walking sluggish and achy. Every station and carriage echoes with a symphony of chronic coughing.

Aboveground, he holds his nose as he passes sheltered stoops and bus stops – the city reeks of neglected bodies, both the alive and the rotting. Their suffering churns guilt and disgust and righteousness at his core. *They need you, Lysander,* he remembers me telling him. *They need your work to free them.*

From a payphone in the cafe's side-street, he uses every coin in his pocket to call allies to his cause. Some hang-up when he utters his name, others entertain him long enough to whisper rebukes.

'We went too far,' says a dancer.

'Lucky we didn't get locked up with you,' says a flautist.

'I have a family to think of,' says the best hand-drummer in the city.

'Too radical,' they call him. As if that wasn't the point. Theatre had lived underground most of Lysander's lifetime. Now they refused visitors to their exclusive burrow.

'But I'm staging *Tender Melodies and Wakeful Fantasies,*' he lies. A tame, conventional show with jokes in the middle and a double marriage finale. 'Nothing mad, nothing dangerous.'

When they hang-up laughing, he slams the phone on the hook. He checks his watch and vows to try more numbers later. Someone will join him.

He enters the cafe. The front door bell tinkles, and the handful of patrons spare him a glance. They shift on squeaky plastic-cushioned seats, but their details smudge, their expressions in shadow. Fluorescent lights bounce off linoleum surfaces and my bald head, where I sit alone in the back corner. Lysander recognises me; he is blind to all else. I hear his thoughts as he squeezes between tables, sweat slicking his spine like condensation on the windows. He thinks I do not fit this scene.

Sleek suit and gleaming eyes, darker than the scratchy scents of burnt bacon and black coffee wafting from the kitchen hatch. Ever-amused quirk at the corner of my mouth, as if I know and enjoy how strange I must appear to onlookers. I look the same as last he saw me – in the Reformation Centre, in his dreams, and before, at the ritual he experienced over-shores. My expression disquiets him more each meeting. Wisely, he tries not to dwell upon its curious eternity.

I stand as Lysander reaches my table and takes the chair opposite. We sit in unison.

It's a greasy spoon, not a formal of ballgowns and fine crystal, he thinks but doesn't say.

He whisks off his cap, mops his brow with it, then twists it in his lap, hoping I won't notice the anxious tick. I sip my tea and wait.

'Am I glad you're here, Amon,' he says. 'Things are...worse. As you expected. It's been a trying day, but they'll come around. We'll make them understand. There need only be a handful for the second run, and once we get started, the rest will beg me to let them in on the performances.'

He calls me by the moniker I gave him – Amon – for my true name upon his tongue would spoil the plan. I nod whenever he speaks, granting him an engaged audience. The first of many, I've promised.

'It is good to see you outside, my friend.' The register I adopt is cashmere and silk – soft and luxurious. Easy, with all the time in the world. It's what Lysander expects from anyone wealthy and brazen enough to fund dissident art. 'Being free agrees with your spirit. You've colour back in your cheeks. You seem more...yourself.'

'Free,' he scoffs. 'This is a paltry excuse for freedom if I can't find souls brave enough to stand up with me. I cannot do this alone. The show needs performers, and a space. And *we* need the show, everyone does. Otherwise we'll keep living this way, under their thumb. We must wake them up, rally them against this drudgery.'

He breathes. I discern in his face how soothing it is to spill his desires aloud, to shirk his charade of normality, in the company of someone he believes is a like-minded soul. For my part, I don't hide my smile at his words. *Wake them up*. He knows not how right he is.

'You still have my support, of course,' I say. 'Perhaps, I could make a few calls?'

He wraps both hands around the steaming mug of black liquid I'd ordered for him, shakes his head. 'No, no. I'll handle the performers. You did plenty, convincing them to release me from Wilde-Welkin early. Another month and my mushed brain would've leaked out my nose. I likely wouldn't even recall seeing your dance show over-shores.'

I freeze, fingers bone-white against the teacup, and wrestle to keep my amused smile on my face. Luckily, Lysander doesn't notice. He searches for answers in his reflection on the drink's surface. When I'm composed enough to speak, not a tremble gives away my concern.

'But you *do* still remember it, don't you?'

He sips his drink and winces at the acidic taste, recalling the medicine they gave him at the Reformation Centre. One drop is enough.

Inside, his mind bursts with powdery, primary-coloured memories. Dancers swaying and jolting and writhing to the clashing-metal music like none he's ever heard before or since. None sing, none speak. Their bodies transmit ancient tales of profound truths direct to his consciousness. Life fizzes through him, tingling as if he wakes from a thousand-year sleep. They snatch him onto their 'stage' and he is part of the rhythm. Someone thumps on the skin of his heart drum. Flutes blow discordant winds up his nose.

In that stone circle, deep in the cave, they spin him in a battering, flailing vortex of human commune. It tastes of sugary citrus and bodily fluids, of purpose and power. He licks his lips and listens as the screams become a ringing in his ears.

The memory dissolves. Lysander rubs his sleeves where the bruises and scars beneath smart. Despite the pain, I perceive resolve flickering anew in his eyes. Tension sheds from my mortal form at this sight, and I grin. He lifts his mug to his lips, but I reach out and lower it.

'I have something for you,' I say. 'For luck.'

From the duffle at my feet, I retrieve the box. He traces the hexagonal sides with his fingertips, studies the impish faces and symbols he cannot read carved in the coarse wood. Language from a time before language. Its great age manifested in every crack. He opens the tarnished metal clasp with a click and gasps.

The gem that lies inside nestles within a coil of gold chain, a protective mother snake around the precious, misshapen egg. There are too many edges to count and a shine to its dark surface that shifts colours with the light – *red, green, yellow, navy, violet, magenta…*

Lysander pinches the necklace and lifts it from the box. A reflected eye, he assumes to be his own, blinks at him.

'From the ceremony over-shores,' I explain. 'Put it on, put it on.'

He obliges, sagging under the surprising weight of it against his chest.

'There, that'll do the trick. We'll have no more obstacles, Lysander. This is your missing piece. Everything will fall into place this time, you'll see.'

***

All Zoe's calls go unanswered. When she stops by Lysander's flat, he's not there. After months of knowing where he is at every hour, his absence is troubling. Any reassurance she'd enjoyed at seeing him, speaking to him, realising he was out in the world, has waned. She prays that his time at Wilde-Welkin proves enough of a deterrent.

Her nightmares persist though he promised not to repeat the performance. There had been no trace of that feverish obsession in him – that mania that kept him up into the twilight hours every night after voyaging over-shores. And yet...

A wrongness wriggles beneath the surface of her skin. It pulls her from her bed in a vice grip of compulsion. She dresses, leaves the flat and wanders along the road, abandoning her car in the tenement's lot. Through the nacreous haze of light pollution, a full moon surveils her from on-high. She ought to be careful, to navigate her practiced route through alleys and residential gardens, one she could follow with eyes closed. Instead, she strides major thoroughfares during curfew and, for the first time, is unafraid how the law might punish her disobedience.

There are worse things to fear. The words are a whisper in her mind, in a voice not her own. A familiar voice.

Am I still dreaming? She asks herself. *No,* she's never had a dream as vivid as this one.

She can *feel* too much. Damp mist raises gooseflesh on her exposed arms, and the night air tangs with lingering exhaust fumes and sewage. Her distressed-denim jacket hangs forgotten on the coat rack at home. She shudders. Now the voice is with her in the waking world too.

Her next blink finds her staring at the old community hall with its greying pebble-dash, smashed glass door, and the sprayed tag of a local gang scrawled across the welcome sign. Such a journey should have taken over half an hour, not minutes.

Why am I here?

There's no light on within. As always, the place appears deserted. Zoe, whose idea it was to have this rough, forsaken exterior, knows better and heads for the real entrance in the alley. She falters when she observes me.

I'm atop the metal fire-exit stairs, leaning against the wall by the door, illuminated by the moon and the orange tip of my cigarette as I drag upon it. She glares at me from the bottom of the steps.

'Hey, this place is closed,' she says.

I toss the smouldering butt, watch it tumble through the grating to the pavement. Then I move into the light so she can see the half-smile pressed on my pale, thin lips. Mocking, amused. I lean on the railings.

'Then what are you doing here?' I reply.

She gasps. *That voice*, my voice, is the one from her nightmares.

Am I dreaming?

No, I say in her head.

Hairs on her nape prickle. She peeks over both shoulders, scanning the brown-tinted glass towers that dwarf the community hall. Anyone might watch from those windows. She's exposed, out after curfew. It's then that she realises I appear governmental with my formal wear and cool assurance. Panic pulses in her blood. She imagines me taking her in, locking her up and—

'—Better get inside, it'll be starting soon.' I yawn and revolve languidly to open the fire-exit.

When the door clangs behind me, I fill her mind with my voice: *Lysander will be so disappointed if you miss it.* She bounds up the stairs two at a time, ignoring their dangerous sway and the creak of rusting metal.

Within, a green emergency sign lights the corridor, but I am gone, not even a silent shade in the gloom. Office carpet dampens her wary footsteps. She follows the murmur of conversation, pulse pounding in staccato, to the last door on the right – her theatre. She knows what she will find there.

Please, she prays, *let me be wrong.*

Standing in the doorway, she slumps against the jamb, a scream bubbling in her throat. She's reversed in time, or fallen into her nightmares. Moonbeams from the skylight paint the scene in stark black and white. A few glimpsed profiles are enough to convince her that the packed audience, facing away from her on function-room chairs, is the same from the dreaded preview night. People she'd whispered with, who'd shared her terrors. They'd returned, come back for more, for a second showing.

As she had. Their milky gazes fix forward on the stage and Lysander's command.

Two crimson sheets, a makeshift curtain, flank him. The gem about his neck shines a rainbow of hues. Near invisible dancers, dressed in black body suits, amass in a regiment behind him, and the musicians wait in the aisles for his signal. When he beckons, the show will go on as if three months had been but an intermission for his theatre of cruelty.

Sour terror tickles Zoe's gullet. She raises a foot to step into the room, to stop this before it begins. Something gloopy resists her, sucking the shoe back to the floor. She tries the other, glances at her feet. Several inches of glistening slime cake the carpet. She's trapped.

I chuckle as she pales and squirms. Her head snaps up and she finds me in the corner.

'No point struggling,' I say, my focus on the performance. 'You've foreseen what's coming.'

And for a brief, idiotic moment, she pictures me – whom she believes to be an odd government official – cuffing her friend and hauling him away for good this time. Flushing with relief, she imagines for a moment that I might cancel the performance. It's when my irises glow white under the moon and Lysander waves an imaginary conductor's baton that she knows. I am no establishment spy.

Shrill metal shrieks shake up her thoughts, tumbling them like a washing machine. The dancers blur in their maelstrom. Lysander's back arches and his mouth gapes in a dumb wail at my gem floating before his face. Its sheen expands and expands to an inky, rippling barrier, touching the ceiling and opposite walls, hiding the performance behind it. Zoe and the audience behold the void. They witness again what they have witnessed here before, and every eve in their slumber for the last three months. But this is no mere vision. It is real. Through the jewel, the gateway opens.

Within the smothering darkness of the barrier, in a miniature night sky, a crisp blue sun crushes against the earth. It flattens everything to rubble, and on that rubble assembles the hooded ones to rebuild it all afresh. They turn upon the audience flaxen eyes of understanding. Lightning cracks the secret theatre's skylight, releases havoc out into the streets.

A rumbling earthquake signifies that *they* have woken. My elder kin. With the ceremony complete, they arise from their long slumber in the void. Someone laughs, perhaps it is me, as the touch of the growing abyssal gate turns those willing victims gathered into convulsing masses of limbs and teeth.

They are free, as Lysander wished. As I had promised. Their fights for and against oppression end. They are returned to chaos, whence everything is formed, to serve a new dream.

The Unkindness of Ravens

Claira Wilson

Overhead they circle, arching against the sky like arrows,
their midnight plumage rustles ink-wet, dripping with a palmful of sorrows,
and like sharp slants of slate they swoop by, haunting all my tomorrows.

The night claims the day with clawed fingers, the rolling summer's day no longer lingers,
giving way to blotting paper clouds, heavy with rain that doesn't yield,
here the ravens gather, hooded and menacing in the dewy field.

Mother, how they rest against your hair, like cinders among the wheat,
so gently they eat from your hands, cawing at the feast of meat,
sitting, waiting for the shadows into which they will retreat.

I worry about the noise from our town, they cry Witch! and I stretch only so far a Crown,
Mother, you have told me not to worry, not to cuss, not to fuss,
though I can't help but wonder what fate will befall you and I should your ravens ever fail
us?

Mother, we are not gifted the same, I must seem tame compared to how you maim,
but I hear the sand that trickles through the black feathers and the stone that weathers,
please, I beg, take my hand and fly, leave behind and cut all other tethers.

I turn for home, weaving in and out of shadows cast long by phantom gallows,
when there is a roar that bellows across the meadows, till it tapers and hollows,
I turn to see Mother look at me, then away toward the ravens she leaps, and follows.

In a flurry of catching darkness, she is swallowed whole, no wisp of gold among the coal,
my heart stills and my legs, strong and able, shake weak like a newborn foal,
Mother mine is not returning, this I know in the very depths of my soul.

How did I not foresee this, this emptiness that so quickly consumed me?
Though the answer is so swift, it's almost missed, and I choke on a sob and a hiss,
I know what I see, Mother has given me a key and now I too can be free.

All those times I thought I was unheard, drowned out by the cawing of birds,
how absurd, how could I have dared to dream she had not cared,
all along she knew how I fared and waited till I was ready and not so easily scared.

The ravens dissolve against a darkening sky, Mother with them flying so high,
if I tell only one lie it would not be that I didn't cry, face wet wishing I could fly,
to join her in skies so bold, longing for my childhood and a warm hand to hold.

I'm a seer of time, committed no crime, not to false Gods or priests with poisoned wine,
yet we are parted and chased, by those who don't know what it's like to be graced,
and when I peer into windows to see we'll never meet again, I feel pain I could not feign.

Mother, though it rends my heart in two, we will go our separate ways,
I will remember your strong hands, your calm gaze, even as my hair greys,
and in these older days, I will, like you, feed the ravens in the late summer haze

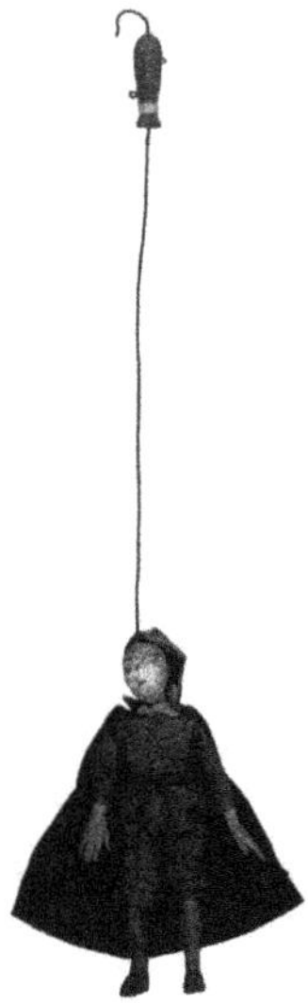

Act V

If we shadows have offended,
Think but this and all is mended:
That you have but slumbered here
While these visions did appear.
And this weak and idle theme
No more yielding but a dream.

A Midsummer Night's Dream V • 1

Tomorrow's Problem

Gabriel Munro

The band ended with a cover of *We Are the Champions*, and it felt true. All evening we'd been simmering in the shimmering mess of it all – the dancing, the glances, Snow's deep laugh and clever eyes. When the house lights came on, we were boiling over, kissing like we were the only people in the room. In time, we were.

When the winter wind whipped us away from the dancehall, Snow held my hand in his coat pocket and said he lived right around the corner. Six blocks. I leaned into him down icy alleys, past hibernating sedans with impenetrable windows, along junkier and junkier front lawns. The night air made me miss my beard and the camo coat I'd convinced myself not to bring to the city.

'This is me,' he said. This was Snow: a rundown apartment building with a hesitant elevator. Neither of us minded. The little metal box coaxed itself through its own vertigo, level by jittery level, until it let us out with a sigh. Snow's keys jangled as he opened door 603 and we spilled in.

'I'm just going to go rinse off,' he said, abandoning me on his messy futon. 'You good out here?' My face was still numb from the wind and the elevator ride, but I tried to smile. He looked back from the bathroom door, tall and underfed and impossibly relaxed. 'Don't let Tommy out, by the way.'

'Tommy?'

'My cat. He's in the closet,' he said, eyeing the closed door across from the bed.

'Why do you keep a cat in your closet?'

'He's kind of a lot.'

With that, he closed the door and started the shower. I collapsed and stared at the ceiling, wondering if it meant anything that he hadn't invited me. The hiss of water was like the sound of a party in another room. Parties were always in another room for me. Up until that night, I'd never even seen a rock concert before. It was a good thing Snow had only known me for three hours; how else could he think I was cool?

I kicked off my boots and peeled off the flimsy pea coat that should've made me look urbane. I tugged his musty comforter around me. I waited.

Snow's apartment was an adolescent ode to autonomy: dirty mugs and paint tubes and books cluttered the desk, a pile of clothes mulled at the foot of the mattress, the walls lifted flags and posters, sketches and paintings. Every face on the glossy posters was young and alluring. Cheekbones jutted, deep dark eyes like warm pools beckoned me to take a dip. The drawings and paintings seemed to be of different fantasy characters, though they all had a Snowness to their faces. He only seemed to know how to draw nervous eyes; they had the warning of haunted wells.

Somewhere, surely, in Snow's future and in mine, there would be a line we crossed into real adulthood. This ragtag apartment would have no place beyond it. But, then, neither would making out with strangers in dancehalls. I closed my eyes and tried to savour the suspense. I could enjoy being the newest object in Snow's clutter. I could be the latest meaningless poster he pinned against his wall. Youth was a sunset, and I was desperate for its warmth.

I pulled out my phone and took a photo, maybe just to prove that I'd been there. I sent it to Ellie.

How's your new apartment already a mess? she texted.

Not mine… I replied.

She sent a string of shocked emojis. *DID YOU MEET SOMEONE???*

I was happy to flaunt my new urban life, my new urban self. I tried to formulate something witty and nonchalant, something the city would want me to say, but my thoughts were interrupted. A loud banging on the closet door tore through the apartment.

This guy must have the world's biggest cat. I sent an audio recording of the half shower hiss, half pounding closet door. *He said not to let him out of the closet, though.*

Poor baby, she wrote back. *Freedom for Closet Cat!*

I tucked my phone back in my pocket. Snow couldn't be long now. How much time did it take to rinse off?

The banging continued. I reached over to turn on the lamp in the corner. I wasn't intimidated by a cat, of course, but it was unsettling.

I lay down, failing to ignore the din.

'Cut it out,' I blurted.

For a moment, it seemed to work. The cat left me to the steady sound of running water.

When the room filled with the scraping of claws on wood, I rose and pulled out my phone again.

He's scratching now, I typed. *It's weird, though. Sounds bigger than a cat.*

Maybe he's hiding something exotic. Freedom for Closet Cougar!

Even from three hundred kilometers away, Ellie made things better. I pictured her glittering smile lighting up the room.

Come to city. We have Closet Cougar. I'd been trying to get Ellie to follow me since I'd first decided to move out. So far, my silly tourist slogans were failing to sway her. She usually changed the subject.

No cougar is free until Closet Cougar is free! she replied.

The clawing was a rickety elevator grating its slow way down to the floor. It sure didn't sound like a tabby. And weren't cats supposed to mew?

'Is it a dog?' I said to no one.

The clawing stopped. I let out a relieved sigh in the silence.

Then the apartment filled with the sound of barking.

I couldn't take it. I knew I was interrupting, I knew it wasn't cool or chill or whatever else I was supposed to be, but I started rapping on the bathroom door. The water stopped.

'Yeah?'

'It's a dog! In your closet, I mean.' I didn't know what I was asking, but I needed an answer nonetheless. 'I thought Tommy was a cat.'

Snow paused, maybe to wonder why he'd brought me home. 'Tommy *is* a cat. Be a cat, Tommy!'

I heard Snow step out of the tub. Then, infuriatingly, the apartment filled with mewing.

I crouched at the closet door, painted cheap-apartment-beige, and listened.

'What are you?' I hissed, hungry for some clue or confession.

Tommy didn't reply, except to resume his banging against the door.

Snow stepped out of the bathroom and smiled down at me. He'd put his faded grey jeans back on but not his shirt. A ratty green beach towel was draped across his shoulders.

'Wutcha doin' down there?' he smiled.

'I, um,' I stuttered as he helped me to my feet. Snow smelled clean, with a hint of shower gel that was probably called *Maximum Sport Burst* or something else that suggested a testosterone factory explosion. His hands felt softer than before. He was still so relaxed.

'Talking to the cat?'

He closed the distance between us. I inhaled.

'Okay, but *is* it a cat?' I blurted, stepping back. 'Because it was definitely barking. And before, it was scratching, but not like a cat. So, like, why won't you just admit you have a dog *and* a cat?'

'Tommy can be a dog,' he offered, 'I just like to think of him as a cat.'

'I don't care if he's a cow, I just – can I see him?'

Snow straightened. 'Please don't bother my cat.'

I could feel the moment wilting in my hand.

'You're right,' I said. 'It doesn't matter.' Maybe I'd heard the neighbour's dog.

He accepted my olive branch and led me to the futon. We sat there, close to each other and getting closer, and then somehow we were lying down, pulled by a gravity that belonged to Snow, not to the earth. I had work the next day, but that was tomorrow's problem.

I'd only ever kissed one person before: my ex, Grayson. I'd thought we'd perfected the art on our first try. Somehow, though, I couldn't remember our last kiss. It's easy to overlook the present when you think there's a future.

Before I had a boyfriend, I'd always thought breakups were optional. If you loved someone, and they loved you, why wouldn't you just make things work? It shouldn't be complicated. Why did expectations and words like *space* and *pressure* hover like vengeful birds of prey?

Grayson and I never knew exactly what to do, so we figured it out with each other. Two weeks on Grindr in this city, though, had me feeling like I'd wandered onto some great stage. There were veteran actors around me, all waiting for me to slip into character, but which character was it? Was I an otter or a twink, a switch or a brat? Was I trans or just gay, and how could anyone just be gay when no one could assume the gender of the bodies they daydreamed about?

And while I tried to give myself over to the careless moment, to the tides and riptides of lust and loneliness, I felt like the stage lights had followed me here, too. How was I to act, and who was I to be?

Then, as if to refute all scripts and roles and declare identity absurd, the animal in the closet mooed.

'That was a cow!' I yelled, sitting up.

'He's a cat!' Snow sang out.

Manners be damned, I spent my childhood surrounded by them – I knew what cows sounded like. I jumped from the futon. Snow tried to grab my hand, but he was too late: I swung the closet door wide.

In the same inscrutable, imperceptible way that the present is always becoming the past, the action of pulling the door open had it closing behind me. And then it was dark. I swung around and banged on the door.

'Snow?'

'You idiot!' He yelled, muffled and distant like a memory. 'Close your eyes! Don't look at him!'

But why would I close my eyes? It was pitch black. I groped around for a knob.

'What's going on?' I called through the door.

'Tommy!' His voice had a false authority, like a brandished toy gun. 'Have mercy!'

I found the lightswitch. If Snow wouldn't illuminate anything, at least I could.

The room I was in was large for a closet; maybe ten feet by eight. The best way to describe the size was that it was perfectly proportioned to fit a cow, as clearly demonstrated by the Holstein that was locking eyes with me.

'Oh, hi,' I blurted. I always said hi to cows when I met them, though I'd never been so surprised to see one. A closet-cow was a very different accoutrement to urban life than I'd ever expected to find. 'Snow?' I yelled, like he could explain it.

'Be a cat, Tommy!' was his only reply.

And Tommy did.

How does a cow become a cat? There was no flash of light to mark the occasion; there was no evolution, no shedding of udders and growing of fangs, there was nothing amazing at all but the fact of it. One moment a cow was breathing gentle gusts of warm air onto me, the next a tuxedo cat stared up with a tilted head, like I was the riddle.

'Snow!' I called, taking a step back from the animal. I wanted to ask him a question, but 'what?', 'how?', and 'why?' all tugged for priority. Each was too simple, too absurdly logical to stand a chance against the wonder I'd beheld. A less useful, yet somehow far more appropriate question elbowed itself to the front of the line. 'What the *hell*?'

'Be a cat, Tommy!' he repeated. He sounded so far away.

'Unlock the door!' I rattled the knob. He didn't say anything, and I was left with what looked like, but couldn't possibly be, a cat.

I waited for it to move, but it just sat and watched me like I had something to give it. How could a temporary cat be so relaxed?

'This can't be real,' I protested. Still, although it was ridiculous, and although my heart pounded like it was locked in its own closet, I had to try it.

'Tommy,' I said like the first astronaut buckling up and hoping for the best, 'be a goat!'

How does a cat become a goat? The same way the goat became a dog when I asked it, the same way that dog next became a chicken, the same way the chicken obliged me when I asked it to be a turtle.

I crouched down to look into the turtle's colourful eyes. If it knew that it was a marvel of the universe and not a turtle, it certainly had a very turtle-like nonchalance about the situation.

I liked turtles, even inexplicable ones, but what about all the animals I'd never seen? Why was I recreating a rural biome after such struggles to escape one?

I began asking Tommy to be anything exotic that didn't run the risk of trampling or eating me. First, he was an aardvark – an animal so strange in appearance that I half suspected that Tommy didn't know what they looked like either. Next, he was a platypus, until I remembered hearing that they were venomous and couldn't reasonably guess which piece of its ludicrous anatomy to watch out for. Nothing happened when I told him to be a dodo. Maybe Tommy couldn't be a bird. But no, Tommy became a parrot quite convincingly.

‘Tommy, be more things,’ the parrot squawked in a seemingly jovial imitation. ‘Tommy, be a friend!’

Was that a request? Did Tommy want to be a person?

An electric sensation pulsed through me, like I was Frankenstein’s monster being galvanized to life. Here there was power in my words, potency in my imagination. Sure, Tommy may have been a poltergeist, but I was the one who could make him anything I wanted. He was a ghost, and I was a god and agency was inebriating. Maybe that made me more akin to Frankenstein than to his monster.

I’d always been defensive of Doctor Frankenstein, even when my entire grade ten class concurred that he’d been arrogant to play with the fires of existence. I hadn’t chimed in because I’d been sick of arguing with teachers and had no allies among my classmates. But wasn’t the answer for why we explore and create simply because we can? The moment Victor could create life, wasn’t doing so as inevitable as the universe creating ours?

Maybe I could have paused to glean some caution from Mary Shelley, but I was excited and fascinated and bewildered and, above all, curious.

‘Tommy,’ I said, like the first astronaut to safely escape the atmosphere who now aimed brazenly at the sun, ‘be a person.’

As the words escaped my lips, I realized I’d violated my own rule against requesting dangerous animals. It was too late.

Tommy became a young man, baby-faced and narrow and charging directly at me. I leapt out of his way as he threw himself on the door. He was horrified, and so was I.

He looked exactly like me.

‘Snow! Please!’ he screamed, banging on the door like a devil. His clothes were mine, his features were mine, but his voice was older, creakier than mine, and his face had a fear I’d never known. ‘Tommy’s going to kill me!’

‘I can’t! I’m sorry!’ came Snow’s voice. ‘Be a cat, Tommy!’

Tommy wasn’t the only one who transformed: he was back to being a cat, and I was now a maniac. I kicked at the door and pounded my fists, demanding Snow tell me why he wasn't letting me out.

'I can't! If I open the door, he'll get out!'

'So you're locking me up with him?'

'I'm sorry!'

The door wouldn't budge. I yelled and swore and kicked and Snow stopped answering. I tried dialing for help, but for all the miles I'd traveled, my phone beeped out the true anthem of my hometown: I was out of cell range. Even my network couldn't reach me here.

I turned and faced Tommy, trying to understand everything I'd seen.

'What the hell are you?' I muttered. He tilted his head, and then changed again.

'Come to city!' It was her voice. It was her choppy DIY haircut, her exploded-crayon-box aesthetic. The face was almost identical, though her glassy eyes stared right through me and the smile was a thousand degrees colder than Ellie's ever could be. 'We have possibility! We have Closet Cougar that sometimes becomes Closet Platypus. You get to choose!'

I wanted to run. I wanted to fight. I wanted to punish Tommy for this perverse impression of the best person I knew, though I could never hurt something who looked so much like her.

'Stop being people,' I growled. 'You're not Ellie!'

'Come to city! Choose your identity – choose your experience – choose your future!'

'Tommy, stop!'

'You have to pick something!' Tommy chirped with her voice. 'That's the game!'

'Fine! Tommy, be a worm!'

Tommy was a fantastic specimen of an earthworm, pink and striated and long. Now it was easy. When I crushed the worm Snow would have no reason to keep me here. I stepped toward

Tommy, lifting my foot as he stretched and curled aimlessly. I wished I'd still been wearing my boots. Maybe there was a less juicy animal I could kill. I could order Tommy to be a mosquito or a fruitfly instead – but then I might have difficulty catching him. I looked down at the worm that wasn't a worm and thought about Mary Shelley. Was destroying life any less of a sin than creating it? Would killing the monster have redeemed Frankenstein? And how could I measure the value of the infinite lives beneath my foot?

'I want to see you, Tommy,' I said. The sun was in range, and I was a space-dazed cosmonaut. 'I want to see what you really are.'

Tommy became a parrot. 'Choices,' he croaked. 'So many choices!'

'No more choices. Everything is *something*. What are you?'

'Tommy, be more things,' the parrot coaxed. 'Tommy, be a friend!'

'Tommy!' I ordered, 'Be yourself!'

The parrot vanished. I looked for what had replaced it, but the room seemed empty. I scanned the floor for some mysterious bug or a new kind of worm or even a dodo. There were only skimpy-landlord-beige walls and a floor that smelled a little like a farm. Soon, the lightbulb dimmed, and darkness thickened around me. There was a chill, like the winter wind outside a dancehall. I felt weak and lightheaded, and I couldn't resist crouching down.

'Where are you, Tommy?' My voice came out raspy. If Tommy could be a big cow, maybe it was fair that I become a little hoarse. I felt breathless. Sleep pulled at me like gravity and my mind roamed around the spinning room. I gazed at my hand as I wondered if oxygen was really worth the effort. My palm looked different. There was a wrinkle I hadn't noticed. Then, there was another. Even the world's worst palm-reader could interpret the symbols of old age.

From sore knees I leapt back up and ran to the door.

'Snow! Please!' I begged. Strength and youth bled from me in rivers. My lungs were failing and my heart was furious and my vision was a sinking ship. 'Tommy's going to kill me!'

'I can't!' he repeated. 'I'm sorry!' How could someone so rigidly selfish have been such a competent kisser? 'Be a cat, Tommy!' he added, but it did nothing.

I turned and faced the darkness.

'Be a cow, Tommy!' I gasped. 'Be a parrot! Be a cat!'

No cat appeared. I hunched over against my own will.

'Be Ellie! Please, be anything! Be a person, Tommy! Be Snow! Be me!'

And there I was. Tommy stared at me, through me, and smiled a smile that didn't remind me of myself. I fell to the ground as he stepped over me. He could have crushed me under his heel like a worm, but he didn't. He tapped on the door instead.

'Snow,' he said calmly. My voice seemed strange on him, like an oversized camo coat. 'I know you're afraid of Tommy. But it's okay. He's gone now, I took care of him. Let's just have fun tonight, and we won't talk about the future at all.'

'You really took care of him?' Snow's voice answered. 'He's really gone?'

I wanted to call out, but my throat could only manage a wheeze.

'He's all gone. I turned him into a worm, and then I crushed him.' Tommy looked down and winked at me. 'Let's just get back to our date. We'll have fun.'

I heard the door unlock. I heard it open and close, and then the sound of voices in the next room. The party was always in another room. I lay in the dark, and as I faded out and away I tried one last sentence, though my hearing and mind were too poor to know if I really said anything at all.

'Tommy, have mercy.'

Unfinished Exit

Claudia Wysocky

I keep thinking
about the time in high school
when you drew
me
a map of the city,
I still have it somewhere.
It was so easy
to get lost
in a place where all the trees
look the same.
And now
every time I see
a missing person's poster
stapled to a pole,
all I can think is
that could have been me.
Missing,
disappeared.

But there are no
posters for people
who just never came back

and you haven't killed yourself
because you'd have to commit to a
single exit.
What you wouldn't give to be your cousin Catherine,
who you watched
twice in one weekend get strangled nude
in a bathtub onstage
by the actor who once
filled your mouth with quarters at
your mother's funeral.

The curtains closed and opened again.
We applauded until
our hands were sore.

But you couldn't shake the image of
her lifeless body,
the way she hung there like a
marionette with cut strings.
And now every time you try to write a poem,
it feels like a
eulogy.

Corrida

Nadine Brito

'Tell me about this bull.' Andres's fingers were soft as they followed the mark that covered the side of her ribs, tracing the jagged lines that spilled towards her bellybutton.

'It used to be redder.' Christina smiled, shifting to her side to face him. 'Morning to you too.'

'Morning.' He grinned and her heart raced as he leant in for a kiss. She wondered if he heard it. How it knocked at her ribcage. If his hand pulsed from the vibrations. Probably just anticipation. He was so warm. So comfortable. And so *right*. It was almost frightening, how right. As he pulled her closer, their kisses lengthened. All her thoughts began to flow away as instinct took over once again.

No. Not now. The alarm bells of logic blared through her mind. Last night was great, but she needed to be careful. Take it slow. Mustering all willpower, she pulled away, breathing deeply as she rested her head on the pillow.

'His name was Islero.'

'What?' His thick eyebrows furrowed. He was in a daze.

'The bull. The one you asked about.' Andres was so beautiful. It felt dangerous to look at him for a long time. She focused on the tip of his ear instead.

'Oh.' He seemed to come to. 'Right. Yes.'

'It was a long time ago. When I was just starting out. I misjudged…was lucky though.'

'And the bull?' He touched her scar again, his hand warm.

'The bull died. He always does.'

'Right.' He paused, thinking. She allowed herself to look at him again, and watched as he opened his mouth. Hesitating, he closed it again.

'What is it?'

'It's – it's okay that I ask about the bull, right?' His voice was serious. Concerned. Not at all what she had been expecting, and she couldn't help the loud laughter that erupted from her.

'Of course you can ask!' she burst out. 'Sorry, I'm not laughing at you, I just – I was expecting you to ask a long time ago.' It'd surprised her that he hadn't said anything in the four months they'd been seeing each other. Most men she dated only ever wanted to talk about her being a matador. Always asking about the corridas, the bulls, the scars etched across her body. Not that there were many to note – good matadors didn't let that happen.

Still, they had their opinions. Opinions and advice that she never asked for. That was why Andres was so refreshing. They could talk about anything and everything, and it all just…*flowed*. From mundane discussions about snack foods to philosophical musings about the meaning of life, she'd never found anyone so easy to talk to before. 'Why are you asking now?'

'I don't know,' he gazed at her thoughtfully. 'I figured since you didn't want me to come to a corrida, it wasn't something you wanted to talk about. You were really firm when you said you don't let guys you're dating watch.' She supposed she had been pretty militant about that rule for a while. It was the first thing she always told men on any first date. 'Why do you have that rule anyway?'

She sighed. 'Guys just…feel a certain way about me doing what I do.' It never mattered that her work had nothing to do with them. *They* weren't the ones facing down a raging beast thousands of pounds larger. *They* weren't the ones who'd spent decades training to grapple with the bull. *They* didn't dance with death as it hurdled at them, knowing that it only took one misstep. No. *She* had chosen the rush of it all for herself. Yet they hated everything they thought her choice said about them.

'You don't have to worry about me. I'm secure.' There was a chuckling glint in his eye. How did he always seem to read her mind? 'And I would like to see you in the arena, you know. See a warrior in action.'

'I'm not a warrior,' she laughed.

'Yes you are. And you're my girlfriend. My girlfriend the matador.' He moved his hand to her hip, giving it an affectionate squeeze. She pursed her lips. 'What is it?'

'Do adults really use those terms anymore?' They'd known this was where it was going, but it sounded weird to hear that word in his mouth. Something about it made her uneasy, and she couldn't quite put her finger on it.

'I'm not calling you my partner,' he wrinkled his nose, '*partner* reminds me of the people at work, and you aren't *them*.'

'I don't like the term girlfriend and boyfriend!' she snapped, instantly regretting it. Why was she trying to pick a fight? There was nothing wrong with either term. Andres was perfectly lovely and he had to call her something. Most women would be thrilled. And she was thrilled. 'I'm sorry,' she pushed her lips into a grin. 'I think I'm still a bit tired.'

'It's okay.' His voice was soft. Soft, and understanding, she didn't deserve it. He reached for her hand, pulling it close to his chest. 'We'll think of something. I could call you *my* matador? Until we think of something better?'

'That'd be nice.' She didn't love it either. It felt so...possessive. And kind of cheesy. But he didn't mean it that way. Not everyone was like that. He was right; they'd think of something better.

'So can I come to see you, sometime? Whenever you'd like,' he quickly added, 'I don't want to be a distraction.'

He'd never be a distraction. Not when she had a bull to face. That was far from her concern. 'You've only ever seen one on TV, right?' He nodded. She bit her lip before speaking. 'It's just – it's a different atmosphere entirely. Some people aren't prepared –

they *know*, but they don't really *know* – it's a blood sport – and aren't you afraid I'll be hurt?' She wouldn't be hurt. Not seriously. But sometimes scratches and falls looked worse than they actually were.

'You won't get hurt.'

'But what if I do?'

'I'll go to the hospital with you and be there while the doctors do their job.'

'You won't try to make me quit?'

'Christina,' his voice was firm. 'It's your world, and you're the expert. I want to be a part of it.'

Oh, he was so perfect. Her heart swelled and her eyes watered. 'Then okay. Yes. You can come.'

'Are you alright?'

She nodded, her face breaking into a radiant beam. 'You're really great, you know?' She leaned forward, her mouth finding his.

'So are you,' he laughed as they shifted, his hand on her thigh as he pulled her closer. 'And this one, from the same bull too?' He asked as his fingers found the small burn scar on her inner leg.

'Oh. From when I was a kid,' she lied. 'Just an accident. Playing with matches.' She pulled him into an embrace, and they ceased talking.

***

'Your *chaquetilla*.' Mariana held the jacket open. Christina lifted her arms, letting Mariana slide it on, then turned to look in the mirror. The red of the silk was as bold as ever, the silver of the threads and sequins shining in the light. She stared at herself, smiling as she checked that everything was in place, that not a strand of hair fell loose from her tight braid. There wasn't really anything to be concerned about; Mariana was excellent. They'd had the same dressing ritual ever since her *alternativa* ceremony, when she became an official matador. Christina liked seeing herself like this. The outfit was beautiful, and she seemed so long and lanky. Graceful. Yet with an air of intimidation. Hearing a sharp intake of breath, she looked to Andres, who stood behind, staring at her in the wide mirror.

'You look…' he trailed off as she turned around to face him. 'So this is one of the famous *trajes*.' Reaching out, he traced the silver embroidery on her shoulder. 'You're very shiny.' He grinned, squeezing her arm. 'Do you get to choose the colours? Or is it some sort of ranking thing?'

'I chose them, I wanted red and—'

'—it is time for her to focus,' Mariana interrupted, her brusque tone meaning business. 'You must go.' The tiny old woman glared at Andres, grabbing his wrist and pulling him away. Christina laughed at his look of confusion; tall and imposing Andres probably hadn't been spoken to like that since he was a boy.

'Mariana is quite superstitious,' she said as he was ushered through the door, 'we have our routine before the show, and it worries her if it is altered in any way.'

'You shouldn't laugh,' Mariana said, 'I'm dressing you to kill, and that is a serious business. It is time for your moment of silence.'

'What's that?' Andres called out.

'I'll tell you later. Enjoy the show.'

'Good luck. I love you.'

I love you. It was the first time he'd said it.

Before Christina could reply, Mariana shut the door firmly behind him. 'You must focus, you shouldn't have brought him back here.'

'Ah, Mariana, I just wanted to show him how I get ready.'

Mariana snorted. 'It's not good to play with fire. It only takes one tiny false move. The next thing you know, the beast gets at you. Then you're lying in a pool of your own blood, and he comes back and tramples over you. Again, and again.'

'As always, a happy picture before I go out.' Christina adjusted her tie.

'It's best you have that image in mind, it keeps you sharp. Everything is good.' She looked Christina up and down once more. 'And you have your hat. Good.' The black montera lay on the dressing table. 'Are you going to dedicate it to him?'

'I don't know. I hadn't thought about it.' It was an overwhelming idea, and she couldn't say why. She'd dedicated it to plenty of audiences before. To the occasional child cheering her on, so excited to be there. Why not dedicate it to him? Toss it to him during the third act? But something about that felt different this time.

'You'll know what to do.' The two women stared at one another in the mirror, and Christina knew Mariana was about to bid her the usual departure words. 'You'll do well today. May luck be with you, and as god wills, I shall assist you after the show.'

'Thank you.' Christina smiled.

'He seems nice,' Mariana said over her shoulder as she closed the door.

Christina continued to grin, wiping at her eyes as tears began to well up. Funny how that happened when things were good and never when they weren't. She really needed to stop doing things this way. Mariana was right. It was her time to clear her mind.

Taking a deep breath, she let everything out. Closed her eyes, and allowed all thoughts to flow away as she went into her meditative trance, where everything became silent and dark.

That was how it was supposed to be. But in the stillness, there was an uneasiness. Deep in the depths of her soul, it spread rapidly the more hushed everything became, quicker than she could manage. She began to tremble as it consumed her entire body.

He loved her.

He, a *good* man, loved her.

A good man, who didn't deserve this uneasiness, loved her.

Was she uneasy because she didn't feel the same way?

No – that was wrong. She was intensely aware that she loved him too. More than she'd ever loved anyone, and the amount of feeling that inundated her was immense. A vast wealth of feeling that it seemed greedy to hold so much of. It was despicable to want him as greatly as she did. To hoard all of him for her.

What woman deserved all of that?

Certainly not her.

'Precisely.' A low melodious voice spoke aloud, then let out a laugh, a threatening note in its timbre that echoed through the room. Christina's eyes flung open. It couldn't be—!

But there was no one there. The dressing room was exactly as it'd been seconds ago, no furniture out of place, her montera in front of her, the drapes on the window still open. The window...hadn't the sun been shining through moments before? She rose, noticing just how quiet everything was. It wasn't right – the dressing room masked the sounds of the arena, but if she paid attention, she should be able to hear the audience. Feel the anticipation in the air, their palatable excitement as they shouted for the show to begin. It wasn't there.

The room felt as though it'd gotten colder. Darker too. The closer she stepped over to the window, the more shadows seemed to emerge as the light rapidly faded. Staring outside, it was black as night. She couldn't see anything, and turning back to the room, she found it swamped in darkness. A chill came over her.

Moments later, hooves sounded outside the dressing room. Hooves that aggressively pummelled the ground, thrashing through the silence so that their clatter was all she could hear. That, and the menacing snorts from the thousand pounds of pure muscle that barrelled down the hallway.

How in the hell had a bull gotten loose? They weren't even kept nearby – a scream interrupted her thoughts. Followed by crumbling rock and banging as large objects rammed together. Another shout in the distance as the bull continued his rampage onward. Christina squared her shoulders. How it got loose could be figured out later.

She needed her tools, which were in the arena. Cautiously she stepped into the hallway. What had happened to the power? The blue emergency lights that lined the top of the walls were on, their dim glow the only way she could see ahead. In the feeble light, she couldn't make out the fine details of the wall decor, nor the furniture along the sides of the hall. Not that much furniture remained. It had been strewn around, broken and in shambles. She moved forward, her hand on the wall, finding spots that had been gored, small bits of plaster and stone sticking to her skin. He'd gone in the direction of the arena, which was fortunate. Hopefully he'd stay there. It'd make things easier.

A snort sliced through the air. She froze, holding her breath as she listened.

Nothing. The darkness pressed upon her, so much so that she felt a wave of nausea. Best she get to the fresh air of the arena. She took another step.

Suddenly she was assaulted by the sounds of hooves echoing in her head. Menacing voices whispered inaudible words that circled around her, overlapping so she couldn't make out what they hissed. But from their malicious tone, she didn't want to know. There was the sensation of warm breath on the back of her neck, and she stumbled forward, trying to get as far away from it as possible. A coarse tail whipped at her arm and she let out a shriek, choking on the pungent musk that filled the air. A mixture of sweat, iron, tobacco – a scent that she didn't want to remember. But the beast didn't care, all he wanted was to overpower her. And he had the upper hand. She was suffocating, drowning on his stench that her defences were powerless against. A wave of revulsion came up in her throat, and she began to choke on that as well. How weak, how useless, how fragile she was. Pathetic really, how she pretended to be strong when she was anything but. Made such a show of everything, while everyone humoured it, knowing that it was all a facade. That truly, she was just a coward. Not good, or kind, or authentic. Maybe some people were fooled by it for a little while, but they always found out. Their scorn, their derision, their anger – she deserved it all. Deserved for everything to end here, alone in the dark.

'Help me!' Through the pandemonium came a voice. 'It has me!'

Andres. She'd recognize him anywhere.

Painstakingly, Christina forced herself forward, the atmosphere pushing in. But with Andres her focus, she moved along through the labyrinth of hallways. It was strange to stumble through them; she'd walked them numerous times before, knew them like the back of her hand. Yet there was something disorienting about them now. Something so confusing as they tapered on and on, never-ending as she felt more and more trapped in their maze. Andres continued to call, guiding her out. As his voice grew louder, she came to the arena, fresh air wafting over her.

'Andres!' She shouted, hurrying through the troupe's gate to the centre of the ring.

It was empty. Stumbling to a stop, her feet crunched against the dirt, the only sound as all went quiet again. There was no bull. No one in the seats either. Turning her head side-to-side, she carefully scanned to make sure she hadn't missed anyone in the shadows of the night. The moon was very bright this evening, its silver light allowing her to see more than in the hallway. She frowned – the corrida began at five. Why was the moon out so early?

'Andres? Where are you?' Her shout echoed as she returned to the gate and grabbed the spare sword they kept there for emergencies. Wielding it, she turned around, drawing in her breath as she caught sight of a shadow standing near the back of the bullring.

A man. 'Andres!' She rushed forward, lowering her sword.

'I knew you'd come looking for him.' He spoke with derision, his back to her, each word dripping with condescension. The melodic voice that she'd heard in her dressing room. 'Never changes how you throw yourself at the feet of any man you're with.'

Christina stopped in her tracks, dread coursing through her. Marcos.

It'd been years. But he wasn't someone she'd ever forget. *Never* could forget. How she tiptoed around him, so careful not to wake the beast, because to wake him would be bad. 'What are you doing here?' Her voice trembled, and she hated herself for it.

'You made a fool of me Christina, with your usual tricks. Running away, after all I did for you. Supporting you,' he sneered.

'Even though everyone knows how ridiculous it is. Had to come and warn the next guy.'

She made herself taller, made her words firm. 'You never supported me. You're nothing like him.'

He let out a snort. 'You're right about that. He's weak. Listen to how he cries.' Suddenly from every corner of the arena Andres's voice rang, calling for help, shouting that he'd been wounded, each call reverberating off of the other as they mixed to create a jumble of fear and confusion.

'Where is he?' she demanded, once again looking to every corner of the arena.

'I'm surprised. You going for this one. But then, what real man would take you.'

'You call yourself a real man!' she spat, raising her sword. 'You haven't even looked at me yet. Turn around and face me, you coward.'

'As you wish, my dear.' He turned, coming closer, towards the centre of the ring. As he walked she heard hoofbeats on the ground, and her arm tensed. *Relax*, she told herself – then he stepped into the moonlight, and she gasped.

The angry amber eyes of a bull glared at her, and the man lowered the ridged horns that protruded from the side of his head in her direction. Still a man, though he had the head of a bull. His sinewy body was large, and from the way he moved, she knew it was pure muscle that could snap her in two if he got her hands around her. It was Marcos's body. She knew it well enough. Her gaze moved to his feet, transformed into black hooves that stomped at the ground in anticipation. Hands that had become claws that curved out, ready to strike. She went cold as she caught sight of a tattoo that branded the inside of his entire left arm.

'Who are you?' She stared at the crisp straight lines of the jagged cross. Her father's tattoo. The one she always saw, right before she felt pain through every bone in her body.

'You know me,' The beast scoffed. 'But then, you never were very bright.' He lunged at her, and she leapt out of the way, just missing him. 'Didn't expect that?' He laughed as she scrambled away. 'Matadors must always be on their toes. I'll be disappointed if this ends quickly. Though not surprised.' He stomped at the ground, getting ready to charge again.

It was time. All the fear, the pain, the anxiety, the sadness, everything that Christina had felt, was feeling, would ever feel – it welled up, taking her over and leaving her with that unbearable burden that tortured every corner of her body and soul. To feel it all, it was too much. Why did *everyone* do this? Always. Every time. Didn't they know that it hurt? But they didn't care. That's why they did it. And she let them. How could she?

White-hot rage coursed through her. She raised her sword.

'Get the fuck away from me.'

And so, their dance began.

Everything fell away as they began their intricate footwork. The moon, the seats, the rest of the arena – it was just her and him, and one of them would die. The beast was out for blood. Formidable, quick and agile, he evaded her strikes as though he knew exactly what she was thinking. He ran at her, full weight hurling onwards like an avalanche, sharp horns and claws aimed, aching to penetrate flesh. But she was equally formidable. She dodged his passes, twisting around the beast at the most vital moments. He was tiring, but from his snorts and the way his tail swatted the air, she knew she was making him angrier.

'Do you really believe that man is for you?' he growled during one of her passes. 'You, who are so unworthy, so undeserving?'

He was trying to distract her. She wouldn't listen.

'You can try and tell yourself otherwise. You know you agree with me.' He got close enough that some of his sweat flicked onto her.

Too close. She needed to focus.

'No man will ever truly love you,' he snarled, his horn stabbing into her left bicep as he passed.

She cried out, nearly dropping her sword as a fierce pain spread like wildfire through her arm. *Never drop your sword*, she scolded herself through gritted teeth. Blood began to drip down her sleeve.

Behind her, the beast's hooves pounded the ground once

more. His final charge, she sensed. Closing her eyes, she thought of Andres, and his words. *I love you*.

When he was a few feet away, she whirled around. Sword drawn, she leapt over the beast, bringing the blade down into his shoulder blades. Blood cascaded through the air as he bellowed, and they both tumbled to the ground.

***

The audience erupted into cheers, the waning light of the sun filling the bullring. Dazed, Christina rose, clutching her arm. Blood poured from it, the red staining her suit a darker shade of crimson. Sweat rolled down her face, and she licked her lips, tasting the saltiness as her glance fell to the dead black bull that lay on the ground a few feet away. A real bull. Horns, a tail, four legs. A large creature that must have been two thousand pounds. Her sword embedded in his back.

Everything was a blur. She knew she acknowledged the crowd, for she felt it when she tried to wave with the bad arm while they threw flowers and chanted her name. Otherwise, she barely noticed as the medics took her aside to tend to it. They said things to her, about how she was very lucky. Only stitches were needed. She mumbled back words that must have sounded normal, because no one reacted oddly. But she didn't know what she was saying, and later wouldn't be able to recall anything from those moments. It was only after Andres was there, wrapping her in his arms that everything seemed to slide into focus.

'That was intense,' he accidentally brushed her arm, then pulled away at her grimace. 'Did I hurt you? I'm sorry.' There was concern etched across his face, and she saw lines in his forehead that she hadn't noticed before.

'I'm fine,' she said, 'it aches. But it isn't the worst injury I've had. Just another scar.'

'Are you sure? It looked like a bad fight. That bull came close so many times.'

'That bull was…more difficult than others.' She bit her lip, staring at her hands. 'I'm sorry. I brought you to a bad one. They're not all like this. How are you doing?'

'I'm fine,' he frowned, 'don't worry about me. You just took on a bull.'

'You're not upset with me?'

'Why on earth would I be upset with you?' His eyebrows knit together in confusion. 'I was so busy watching you, and you looked so...' he faltered as he searched for the word. '...I could never do what you just did. Do I seem upset?'

'No. I'm being stupid.' She shook her head. 'So you'd watch another one?'

'Of course,' he grinned, then hesitated. 'Why...why are you with me? I'm so...boring. No where near capable of outrunning a bull.'

'I love you.' The words fell out of her mouth before she had time to think. 'You, well, said it earlier, and...' she trailed off as their lips found each other.

A moment later Andres broke away. 'I forgot.' He reached for the bouquet of roses that lay on the bench beside them. 'I brought these for you. It's a custom, isn't it?'

'Yes. Thank you.' She took them as a medic came to check her arm again.

'I knew you'd be okay,' Andres said. 'It's what you do. The bull – it always dies, no matter what, right?'

She nodded. Yes. The bull died in every match. Almost always.

Then there was her. The matador. Always the one meant to walk away. And in spite of everything, she always had. Always would.

But it was important to remember that it only took one.

Breathing in, the sweet scent of roses enveloped her.

After the Rescue

Emily Arnold-Fernández

Sometimes I miss the dragon –
the forked tongue always blunt,
truth-telling that would cut you
and bleed clean, the certainty
of always knowing where you stood.

I miss the moods, transparent
like the steam that mellowed
from between the scales to warm
the wet cave, or the flames that dried
the walls and scorched my arms.

Even the anger was cleansing – clear
like a burn running down a mountain,
then gone like a stone dropped in a bog, no
echoes, just a newly made present
born free from sin. We began again.

When the prince came I spread my arms
wide in front of the soft stomach,
wished I were tall enough to guard
the weak eyes. I went willingly
to save them, this beast so naive.

I went confidently, believing I could keep
my truth. I thought the brand and thrust
of hot iron would cease when I learned
the turns of the next dance, the idioms
to say what I did and didn't mean. Now

wreathed in chains instead of smoke,
I dance so prettily, speak gently, pretend
I've never smoldered. I dream
of caves and the days

I thought the dragon was naive.

Swansong

Ailsa Fraser

Cordelia had outgrown the urge to push aside the red curtain and peek at the gathered audience years ago, but today was different. She was always nervous before a concert; that was nothing compared to the hairball of terror that had choked her lungs. Even the violin wasn't the same, too heavy for comfort, and for a moment she regretted not rescuing her own from the carnage.

So, she gave in and allowed herself the briefest of glimpses. The Riverside Opera House was full of soldiers, the dark, plush seats blotted out by their scarlet uniforms. George would mock her for comparing it to a sea of blood – she never did like cliches – but considering the events of the past week, Cordelia thought she could forgive a lack of creativity. The image, either way, was unpleasant.

Despite its unfamiliar weight, she did her best to draw strength from the violin in her hand. Its carved head, the blindfolded face of the goddess of love, dug its ridges into her skin; pursed lips pressed against her palm like a good luck kiss.

Strength didn't come. Only tears. She did her best to blink them back.

A heavily accented voice snapped her attention away from the audience. 'Are you ready?'

Cordelia let the curtain fall closed.

She turned and faced the woman in charge. What her name was, she didn't know – she just knew she was the wife of one of the leading generals who'd invaded the city, and that she had come with him on his campaign. She was no stage manager. Just the best the invaders had been able to source at such short notice. None of their own talent had wanted to travel to their newly captured city when pockets of it still burned.

Cordelia inclined her head, keeping her voice steady even as it threatened to waver. She had to be the consummate professional here. 'I am.'

Most of the musicians had been dragged to the opera house. Cordelia had volunteered, pretending sympathy, sycophancy, and the urge to survive. The general's wife had accepted it gladly – better to have one willing performer even if the others had been coerced – and she needed as many as possible. This was already the third day of performances, eclectic and mixed, that she'd scrounged together for the armies to enjoy. Bored soldiers were dangerous for everyone, not just innocent civilians. The general wanted them entertained now the killing was almost done.

Cordelia hated simpering. Her limbs shook from it all, but she forced them still. She had no desire to perform for them, with her violin or with her actions. But she had to find George. If George had hidden anywhere when the walls fell, it would have been in the opera house she knew so well. There had been no sign of her so far, but Cordelia had to keep looking.

So, she smiled at the general's wife as she took her position backstage. The other performers, a strange mesh of the city's surviving musicians, shot her disdainful looks for her acquiescence, but she ignored them. She was the only one of them who didn't have an armed escort to seize them if they tried to run. After she'd been helped into her dress and had her hair styled with pretty gold rings, she'd had the run of the opera house – and she'd run all the way along it, until sweat soaked her new red dress, the soles of her feet ached, and her lungs clawed for air. She didn't know its back alleys and corridors half as well as George did, but she'd called her name and prayed she would come.

She hadn't. Cordelia had returned to the wings, had to hastily check her hair was still intact, and had to continue to pretend she wanted to be here.

George had to be here somewhere. If she wasn't here, she was probably...

Cordelia would search again after the performance.

Perhaps the performance itself might even help. George had always been able to tell when it was Cordelia playing, rather than another member of the ensemble. With any luck, she would hear the music and come running.

All Cordelia could do was smile at the other musicians. They looked away in disgust.

There were a dozen of them in total, standing like wayward scarecrows in the wings. It was a strange mesh of surviving musicians: pianists, flutists, a bassoonist, a cellist, and several holding brass instruments. Even a handful of opera singers huddled together, trying to draw strength from their friends' presences. There might be enough different performances to last today, but tomorrow the general's wife would have to go out and find something different. Something to keep the crowds entertained. Cordelia knew she was running out of performers.

A pianist went up first. Their performances trickled past with the hours, one at a time. Cordelia smiled when Jonathan, the cellist, stepped up, but he avoided her gaze. That stung. He had been a friend of her father's. Still, she hummed along to his performance. Excellent as always.

The stagehands buzzed around as necessary, and Cordelia kept a sharp eye out. George had worked as a stagehand for years now; she knew the building inside out and could hide indefinitely, but her colleagues might know where she was. The stagehands kept their heads down, though, and Cordelia recognised none of them. She doubted they would divulge George's hiding place to a stranger.

'Where are you?' she murmured to herself, a breath too soft to even pass her lips. They didn't live far from each other, but on the day the walls came down, Cordelia had found her quarters empty, George already gone. Perhaps she had fled; perhaps she had run to find Cordelia in turn. If so, she would have found out why Cordelia had been unable to stay in her father's music shop.

Days had passed, but she still felt the shock in her body, like someone had laced her veins with gunpowder and touched a candle to her chest. It had hurt then, and it still hurt now, although she tried to push through it and...pretend. Pretend she hadn't found her mother skewered on the pavement outside their shop, her old and rusted rapier useless on the cobblestones beside her. Pretend she hadn't been able to tell that her father had thrown himself in front of his wife in a vain attempt to protect her. He had not been a soldier once, as she had, but he had loved her. He had tried.

Pretend she didn't want everyone in the audience dead.

Cordelia was no soldier either, but she had to find George.

'Where *are* you?' She thought her voice might break if she spoke loud enough for even her own ears to hear. None of the stagehands were familiar to her, most of them young and scared – new recruits? Forced conscripts? – and Cordelia would not torment them by putting them under more pressure.

Until Alice, that was.

A short woman with even shorter red hair, she never blended into the background well, even all in black. Now she flashed like a beacon. When she saw Cordelia, she balked and glanced around, jaw tightening.

Cordelia reached for her. 'Alice. Have you—'

'Good to see you alive,' Alice said shortly, then turned to go.

But Cordelia caught her wrist. 'Have you seen George?'

'Quiet!' the general's wife called.

Alice hesitated. 'She's not with you? She said she was going to find you.'

Cordelia's hands were trembling now, and she couldn't stop it. 'She didn't.'

Alice bit her lip. 'Then I think she's—'

'She's not.'

‘Where else could she have gone?’

‘She’s not dead, Alice!’ But Alice had got free and backed away. Cordelia could only fling the words after her.

‘You’re next.’

She spun. The general’s wife was looking at her sourly. The latest melody – the pianist’s – was dying out. Something in Cordelia’s chest was dying with it.

As the pianist made his escape, the general’s wife fluffed her hair and stood up straighter, ready to stride onstage. ‘Come on when I declare your name,’ she said shortly.

Cordelia watched her go and listened to her speech. She didn’t speak the language of the invaders, and it sounded too musical to carry the bloody instructions it had. If nothing else, the general’s wife was a good orator.

It didn’t help. Even from the wings, Cordelia could hear the whispers and snickers of the distracted audience. They were bored – bored by the performances, bored by peacetime, and bored by the city from which they had been promised so much wealth. She doubted she would do much more to engage them. There was no energy left in her.

She looked down at her hands. They still trembled. Closing her eyes, she took a deep breath, and went still. Her fingers brushed the head of the violin. The carved head of the goddess of love was smooth under her skin.

George might still come. George always followed the sound of her music.

One last song, for George. One last call.

Even if she didn’t know the language, she heard her name in the cascading syllables, and the flourish that the general’s wife gave at the end of her announcement was unmistakable. She strode onto the stage with power, presence, and a grace that had been trained into her for two decades. When she stood on that stage and bowed, no one looked at her. Heads were turned and bent to each other, none to her. The crackle of their chatter was like flames eating through a thatched roof. No one was watching.

She performed anyway.

The violin was heavy in her hands. It was her mother's, handmade by her father as a wedding present. Every violin in her father's shop had probably been destroyed by bored soldiers, including her own, but she'd saved this one when she ran. It had been the gift that convinced her mother to retire from the army and take up a safer life – at least, that had been the intent. The goddess of love, blind as love itself, had been a natural decoration to crown such a gift. Cordelia had never heard an instrument sing so sweetly.

She lifted it to her chin now, and played.

Despite knowing that only the general's wife watched her, she kept her back straight and her flourishes graceful. She played as well as she ever had. The music started low and soft, barely rippling through the cacophony of conversation. She let it build.

Heads turned to glance at her, then away again. She swayed like a willow in the breeze. The dress the general's wife had sourced for her was the same red as their uniform, and it clung to her skin too closely for comfort. It dripped off her in crimson and gold. Between that and the golden rings twisted into her dark hair, she knew she cut a striking figure. When the music loudened – grew faster, more frenetic – eyes turned to her and stayed.

She did her best to scan those faces, even as her fingers danced. She knew none of them. Her chest seized.

Where was she?

Cordelia knew she had lived a gentle life. She had been able to train as a musician, successful and supported, with parents that loved her. She had been blessed with the love she had found in George. But it had been months of siege before the walls fell. It had been nearly a week since the invasion. George was the only person she had left.

George had been the only person she had left.

Now, there was nothing.

She played louder.

Her arms pumped with longer strokes, but the speed of her

song didn't let up. She kept that terrifying pace, the anxious build. Her arm ached. The general's wife was watching her, mouth open. In horror or in awe? Disgust or admiration? She had no time to find out. The music was still climbing. It rang off the rafters. It was going to bring the roof tumbling down. Soon, everyone in the city would hear it.

Everyone except George.

Her fingers trembled, but she harnessed it to make her vibrato ever more powerful. The notes soared, high and low, echoing across this vast room until she thought that even if she closed her eyes, she could map out every detail just by the sounds ringing back to her. The thousands of watching soldiers. The boxes draped in the wealth of armies. The arched ceiling, painted to mirror the heavenly palace of the gods, where the goddess of love herself lived.

Something gripped her muscles. Something else settled around her shoulders, soft but bitingly cold. It felt like the wings of a dead bird. It felt like a shroud.

She couldn't stop playing, her heart so tight she thought she would die. Her arms kept swinging, her fingers twitching, and the noise swelled. A man in the front row stood up and shouted – but she couldn't hear him. No one could hear him.

If George was not here – if George could not hear *this* – she was dead.

Grief tried to puncture the otherworldly hold on her body. Closing her eyes, she huddled into that hold, letting the cold comfort her where there was nothing else. Nothing but the heaving of her muscles, the pain in her chest. Her cheeks were hot and wet, drenched in the thickest and stickiest tears she'd ever cried. The violin strings flashed behind her eyelids as she played a note so high she felt it drill into her skull. She held it, as long as she could, through the thundering pain. Then she played it again – high and screeching and no longer beautiful. With it, she screamed.

Something shattered.

The music silenced, swiftly executed. When she opened her eyes, they were dry. She had not been crying at all.

A sea of blood had appeared before her.

The man who'd stood up, who'd tried to shout, was sprawled in the aisle. His chest was a shattered cavity. She couldn't tell where his red coat ended, or his rent flesh began. Everyone in the front row, in fact, was slumped in their seats. Some had chunks torn out of their chests like their lungs had exploded. Some were missing their heads.

How loudly had she played?

She lifted her gaze. The carnage echoed across the room. Bodies upon bodies lay in the seats. When she looked at the general's wife, she too had exploded. Her beautiful white dress was drenched in dark blood.

Cordelia collapsed to her knees. Instinct cradled the violin against her torso like a newborn, like the only thing she had left. Sobs tore up through her lungs and out of her mouth, and she curled over, shuddering. Still, she didn't cry. When she wiped her cheeks, she found that the wetness was blood.

Caught in the furore, she hadn't even felt it splash her.

The silence rang louder than anything else. George hadn't come. George wasn't here.

George was gone.

That was where they found her. Hunched over in the centre of the stage, a single light shining down on her. Speckled with the blood of soldiers, she still held her violin tight.

The face of the goddess atop it was displayed now; the blindfold had slipped down to her neck. Her expression was twisted in pain, but most noticeable was the mouth. It hung open in a silent scream.

Curtain Call

All the world's a stage,
And all the men and women merely players;
They have their exits and their entrances...

As You Like It II • 7

Acknowledgements

Shadows on the Stage would not have been possible without the support and guidance of several individuals and organisations. They have all contributed in a multitude of ways – whether through providing their time, talent, resources, and/or coffee, we are immensely thankful. They are why you hold this anthology in your hands right now, and we would be remiss not to mention them.

First and foremost, we'd like to thank The Forest and Ryan Van Winkle, as well as the vibrant artistic community that has formed around The Forest through its decades of existence. They have provided the means that have allowed us to focus on the creative vision and editorial work of *Shadows*. Their support has been indispensable, and we are honoured to publish under the Forest Publications banner and continue the work of The Forest into the future. An additional thanks to Olivia Thomakos for being an amazing resource and for her encouragement through the publication process.

To our talented and wonderful creative team made up of writers, poets, artists, and photographers – Alice Eaves, Charlie Hilton, Ethan McOustra and Salvör Sólnes – we are lucky to work with you, and thank you for coming along on this journey.

A big thank you to the wider Edinburgh literary and artistic community for their support and promotion of this project, and a special shout-out to Embassy Gallery for their helpful and appreciated assistance. Many thanks as well to the Firecracker Department for their support from abroad.

To our families and friends who have been there for us through this entire process, thank you for always being there to listen and provide insight.

Finally, to our wonderful writers from around the world – thank you for providing your talent to *Shadows*. We are honoured to have worked with you, and are excited to share your stories.

Nadine Brito and Claire Wallace,
Editors-in-Chief

About the Editors & Contributors

Emily Arnold-Fernández (she/they) is an immigrant from California who now lives in rural Scotland with books, a spouse, and a three-legged cattle dog. In a previous life, she founded the refugee human rights organization Asylum Access. Her recent poems appear or are forthcoming in Cordite, Thirteen Bridges, Aeos and Edinburgh Poetry Magazine. She tends to live on islands.

Bob Beagrie (he/him) is a widely published poet living in Middlesbrough. He has published numerous collections and his work has appeared in international journals and anthologies.

Emry Beattie (he/him) is a poet and author from Glasgow, Scotland. Graduating with a Philosophy M.A. in 2021 from the University of Glasgow, his work largely deals with mythology, fantasy, horror, death, and philosophy. He regularly performs live at open mic nights in Glasgow and Edinburgh. In September 2024 he released his second book, The White Stag, an epic poem set in Celtic mythology about a hero's journey to the otherworld. The White Stag and his other works are released through his publishing company, Sea and Sky Publishing. Besides writing and performing, Emry works as a chef, reads tarot cards, and plays the jaw harp.

Fiona Black (she/her) attended drama college in Scotland and won a scholarship to study for an MA in the USA. She worked there as an actor before moving into film and television production. Fiona was involved in numerous well-known productions from Casualty to Last Tango in Halifax. She took time off from her career to gain an MA in Creative Writing at the University of East Anglia, and now concentrates on writing. Her ten-minute play Just William was chosen for a rehearsed reading by InMotion Theatre company and her play Be Careful won the June award 2021 from London Playwrights. Now living in the Highlands, she organises monthly play readings for new playwrights and made a short film, Mary's Missing. The film illustrated a crown of sonnets she wrote about a missing girl. These poems were later heard on Radio Scotland. Recently, she wrote and directed the play Super Seniors Keep Fit Club which reached the One-Act Play National Final 2023 and is due for radio transmission by Grey Hills production company. Fiona has poems published by PEN, in the anthology Uncovered Voices and in Guardian of the Gateway. She writes film and theatre reviews for The Wee Review.

Nadine Brito (she/her) is a Canadian writer based in Scotland. She writes fiction in the forms of prose and screenplay, usually within the genres of gothic horror and magic realism. She has forthcoming work with the horror podcast Thirteen. Previous work can be found in Middleground Magazine, Origin Stories, From Arthur's Seat, and Short Fiction Break. She is the current co-chair at Forest Publications in Scotland and Managing Editor with Radical Bookshop in Canada. She holds a creative writing degree from the University of Edinburgh and a film degree from York University. Prior to her time in Scotland, she spent a decade working in the Canadian film industry. Find her at https://www.nadinebrito.com.

Barlow Crassmont (he/him) has lived in the USA, Eastern Europe, Middle East and China. When not teaching or writing, he dabbles in juggling, solving the Rubik's Cube, and learning other languages. He has been published by British Science Fiction Association, Wilderness House Literary Review, Sudo Journal, and in the upcoming 41st edition of the anthology Writers of the Future.

Alice Eaves (she/her) is a writer & PhD researcher at the University of Edinburgh, originally from Blackpool, England. She is Editor of the translated poetry collection Tiny Flames: Voices from Ukraine, featured on BBC Scotland. https://www.aliceeaves.wordpress.com

Marco Etheridge (he/him) is a writer of prose, an occasional playwright, and a part-time poet. He lives and writes in Vienna, Austria. His work has been featured in over one hundred reviews and journals across Canada, Australia, the UK, and the USA.

His story 'Power Tools' was nominated for Best of the Web for 2023. 'Power Tools' is Marco's latest collection of short fiction. When he isn't crafting stories, Marco is a contributing editor for a new 'Zine called Hotch Potch. In his other life, Marco travels the world with his lovely wife Sabine. Website: https://www.marcoetheridgefiction.com/

Ailsa Fraser (she/her) is a queer, autistic writer of fiction, non-fiction, and anything else she might try her hand at one day. A recent graduate of the University of Edinburgh, she is currently studying for a master's degree in Environmental History at the University of St Andrews. Her fiction has been published in various student journals and in Forest Publication's previous anthology, Origin Stories. Her non-fiction writing, including pieces on history and the environment, can be found in various mediums online.

Lily M. Frenette (she/they) comes from Minnesota and was raised by the woods and waters. She writes at the intersection of nature, magic, art, and community. They enjoy working in multiple mediums, including: photography, painting, audio, printmaking, participatory experiences, and crafting. Currently, she's at work on a novel called Ghost Town, USA about a town overrun by ghosts and tourists, a family torn apart, cults, art as therapy, and youth in revolt; they are open for representation. Lily graduated with a BA from Sarah Lawrence College and an MSc in Creative Writing with Distinction at the University of Edinburgh. They founded Alba Writing Club. She lives in Scotland with her familiar, the most fearsome cat criminal, Outlaw.

Charlie Hilton (he/him) is an Edinburgh based poet.

C. H. Lei (he/him) now lives in a forest on an island, but left his heart in San Francisco. When not writing about murder, things that go bump in the night, and how confusing it is living as a mixed-racial person, he works as a professional business assistant for a former banking and Fortune 500 executive and occasionally babysits a tortoise.

Lis Maestrelo (she/her) is a Brazilian writer based in Calgary, Canada. She has an Honours degree in journalism and a passion for telling stories. When she is not writing, she tries to make sense of the world through art and photography. Her fiction has been featured in The Dark Winter Magazine, Razzle Dazzle Cafe, and in the anthology Tales From The Kitchen. You can find more about her at: https://linktr.ee/lismaestrelo

Rory MacCallum (he/him) is an insanely committed writer who writes, frankly, because he has to. Whether disaster or glory, he has written novels, plays, short stories and poetry. His novel, Coronis, is available to purchase on Amazon at the Kindle store.

Jo ***Marjoribanks*** (she/her) is a Scottish writer who works in the publishing industry. She uses storytelling as a way of exploring the complexities and challenges of her mental and physical health. What she loves most about writing is its power to create connection and community with people who share similar experiences. She has been previously published in Prosetrics: The Literary Magazine and the Apocalypse Chronicles anthology from Almond Press.

Eleanor McMahon (she/her) is a queer Scottish writer and actor based in Edinburgh. She graduated from Edinburgh Napier's Acting and English course in 2021. Her writing includes Result, which was performed as a staged reading at Edinburgh Napier in 2022, Strays, performed by Broken Bottle Theatre at the Edinburgh Fringe in 2023 and Na'amah and The Boat, which was nominated for the David McLennan award in 2024. Her newest work, The Stars and After, was commissioned by Strange Town and will be performed as part of their 2025 summer season. She is on X @EllieMcM1.

R. M. McRitchie (she/her) is a speculative fiction writer from Scotland. She is a member of the Edinburgh Genre Writers group and most loves folklore, historical fantasy and stories that mush genres together in unexpected ways.

Gabriel Munro (any pronouns) is a Canadian writer and composer who searches for melody within words and story within music. His writing has appeared in Literally Stories, Haunted MTL, and Broken Pencil Magazine. He has twice won Gold in Blank Spaces Magazine's Write Prompt Challenge. He lives in Edmonton, writing radio ads and helping Start With Mothers spread education around the globe. His various artistic projects can be seen at https://www.GabrielMunro.ca.

Megan Nicholls (she/her) just graduated with her master's degree in English Literature and is currently working in the North East of England. Her favourite genre to write is fantasy. Alongside the occasional short story, she is currently working on writing her first novel. She is on instagram @megsbooksandreviews.

Sofia Reyes Valencia (she/her) is a queer, Mexican-American woman based in the U.S. She is a recent graduate of the Creative Writing program at the University of Edinburgh and has previous publications with The Skinny Magazine as well as the University of Edinburgh. She likes writing about horror, the past, and unlikeable women.

Milly Sweeney (she/her) is a poet, playwright and performer based in Glasgow, Scotland. Her work explores queerness, class disparity and mental health, as well as life as a young person coming of age in one of the UK's most vibrant cities. Milly is the most recent recipient of the St. Andrew's Playwriting Award, and her work has been featured at the Edinburgh Fringe Festival as well as in The Stage Magazine.

Olivia Thomakos (she/her) is a teacher and writer from Ohio. She is author of Love & Other Cancers from Stewed Rhubarb Press. Her poem 'What You Wish For' won the 2022 Grierson Verse Prize. Her work can be found in Berfrois and Gutter Magazine among others. https://www.oliviathomakos.com

Douglas Thompson (he/him) is a former Chair and Director of the Scottish Writers Centre and has published more than 20 novels and collections of short stories and poetry from various publishers in the UK, Europe and the Americas, including The Brahan Seer from Acair Books (2014) and most recently Retrovival from Elsewhen Press (2025). He won the Herald/Grolsch Question Of Style Award in 1989, second prize in the Neil Gunn Writing Competition 2007, and the Faith/Unbelief Poetry Prize in 2016. https://douglasthompson.wordpress.com/

Claire Wallace (she/her) graduated from University of Edinburgh with an MSc in Creative Writing. She is a freelance writer and currently co-chair of Forest Publications in Edinburgh. Claire was born in Los Angeles, California, and spent three years in Japan teaching English. She enjoys traveling and exploring bookstores around the world. She is working on a series of urban fantasy stories inspired by the cities where she has lived. You can usually find her writing in cafes, especially when it is raining.

Claira Wilson (she/her) is an amateur poet and artist, creating in her spare time. She finds inspiration for poetry in all corners of life, from her office job to hiking in the mountains of Scotland. Nothing is boring, and there is nowhere a muse cannot be found.

Claudia Wysocky (she/her) is a Polish writer and poet based in New York known for her diverse literary creations, including fiction and poetry. Her poems, such as 'Stargazing Love' and 'Heaven and Hell', reflect her ability to capture the beauty of life through rich descriptions. Besides poetry, she authored All Up in Smoke, published by Anxiety Press. With over five years of writing experience, Claudia's work has been featured in local newspapers, magazines, and even literary journals like WordCityLit and Lothlorien Poetry Journal. Her writing is powered by her belief in art's potential to inspire positive change. Claudia also shares her personal journey and love for writing on her own blog, and she expresses her literary talent as an immigrant raised in post-communism Poland.

www.ingramcontent.com/pod-product-compliance
Ingram Content Group UK Ltd.
Pitfield, Milton Keynes, MK11 3LW, UK
UKHW042042200625
459915UK00003B/6

9 781907 811036